Dedicated to my mother and father.

"Blur Havok" contains intense language, graphic depictions of violence, mild sexual content, and references to disturbing and distressing situations and dispositions. Reader discretion is advised.

Also, "Blur Havok" contains what Wikipedia defines as "a colloquial term used in African-American Vernacular English". This term is used throughout this novel and is not meant to shock, offend, or harass anyone. It is merely used for the sake of authenticity in character dialogue.

Blur Havok 2

The Nexus Campaign

Failus E. Washington

Letter to the Reader

Dear reader,

Another year, another NaNoWriMo.

I'm thankful that we've met again and you're still here, reading my stories. But even with an audience of one, I feel satisfied when I finish another tale. Until the Blur Havok Universe has no more stories to tell, you and I will continue to live in it.

In regards to this novel: this book was the story I wanted to write last year.

So much of who I am now came from the lessons, emotional lashings, and tribulations that came from learning the harsh truths of reality. And I poured all of my scarred, hurting soul into this book. Loud laughs in the morning recalling something funny one of the characters said. Tears falling in the midnight hour as my heart ached over the tough decisions. Long, one party discussions about the logic of a scene while taking a shower.

It's been over a year for me since the last time I've spoken to you. Well, at least in my time.

So I'll say it again: from the bottom of my heart I say – thank you. For reading my novel, for continuing the adventure, and for watching me bear my soul and vulnerabilities.

You make it worth it.

I hope you enjoy.

Failus Washington

P.S.: I made it to 50,000 words *before* this letter. Nothing to cheese this time!

Chapter 1

A lean, black male strode along the dirt path, decked out in blue armor. Thick, dark red stripes decorated his chest plate and a layer of Kevlar covered his thighs, biceps, and abdomen. Dark red fabric that matched the streaks on his chest were connected to his armor at the hips, which flowed behind him as he walked through the ghetto. His thick, metal plated chest was puffed out confidently, silently commanding respect from those he passed.

A street fight broke out between two robotic beings. Ski'tal, they were called – a fairly recent addition to the vocabulary of the people in Valhalla. Some humans dismissed this name entirely and preferred to call them Synthetics, a far more derogatory term. The two Ski'tal drones slammed each other's faces into the gravel road. They shoved each other around, bouncing off the sheet metal walls of the makeshift buildings.

The man turned his head towards the fighting duo, his dreadlocked ponytail swinging behind him. He chuckled out of amusement, his brown face creasing at the sight of the scuffle. He reached out with his clawed, armored hands and pulled the pair of Ski'tal apart. He easily lifted the two up to his eye level by their metal collars. His vivid red eyes watched as the pair tried to swing at each other.

"Alright," he started. "What's going on this time?"

“He's a limped-dick, sack of shit, that's what's going on!” one of the Ski'tal snapped, his ant-like mandibles moving as he talked.

The other Ski'tal chuckled and pointed one of his three fingers at his own chest. “That's not what your girl tells me...”

“Oof.” The black male chortled. “I mean at least he didn't *actually* —”

“She broke up with me last night, you dick!”

The man’s face contorted as he tried to contain his laughter.

“You think this is funny?” The Ski’tal turned his anger towards the human.

“Don’t get mad.” The man shook his head from side to side in a playful way and grinned, his bright white teeth sparkling in the sunlight. “But yes, I do.”

The humiliated Ski'tal growled loudly and clawed at him. The man let go of the adulterer and punched his attacker square in the face, flattening him on his back. The human man scratched his goatee. “Keep the change,” he said flatly before walking off.

Dazed, the fallen Ski'tal sat up and watched his assailant walk away completely unscathed. “You’re a real bastard, Alastor!” he slurred. “Screw you!”

"No thanks, I'm spoken for," Alastor spat back jokingly. As he walked away, his forearm vibrated. He raised it up and read the screen: *Melonie Sanders.* "Speak of the Devil..." he said with a warm smile. He tapped the screen with a clawed finger and a hologram of a fair-skinned young woman projected out of his armored forearm. She had a full head of black hair that fell down to her shoulders, black framed glasses, and a small mole on one of her round cheeks. Her pink eyes observed Alastor lovingly. "How's it going, babe?" Alastor spoke in a soft, suave voice.

Melonie giggled. "Why are you talking like that?"

"Talking like what?" Alastor's voice deepened.

Melonie laughed loudly. "Stop! What is that?" She continued to laugh uncontrollably.

"Does the sensual sound of my luscious voice not speak to your..." he paused for dramatic effect. "womanhood?" Alastor softly chuckled.

"Alastor!" Melonie continued to laugh, her cheeks turning pink.

"Alright, alright." Alastor returned to his normal voice. "What's up?"

"I just wanted to see how you were doing." Melonie smiled warmly. Her mature, warm voice sounded like rich, melted chocolate to Alastor.

"Aw. Thanks, babe. You know I appreciate you, right?"

Melonie blushed vibrantly. She smiled, her perfect white teeth gleaming like the Valhallan snow.

"There's that smile," Alastor said softly. "I've dreamed about—" A large Ski'tal swung a massive sword down at Alastor. "Krag!" Alastor yelled as he sidestepped the gargantuan sword. "The hell, man?"

"Out of my way, puny human," Krag bellowed. The hulking behemoth of a Ski'tal slung his sword over his back and strode past Alastor on all fours.

"You still owe me!" Alastor pointed at Krag. "You big bitch," he calmly muttered, shaking his fist in contempt. He looked back at Melonie on his forearm with a goofy smile. "As you can see, Krag's a very nice guy."

Her perfect smile had faded and she was visibly shocked. "Well, be safe out there," she said softly. "Hey, have you used the shield I had Ozzi make for you?" Melonie asked, raising an eyebrow.

Alastor looked down at his left forearm, where a large mound of compressed silver metal plates amassed in an objective eyesore. "Uh... *Je ne comprends pas?*" Alastor laughed awkwardly.

"Alastor, use the shield," Melonie bemoaned. "You don't have to carelessly throw yourself around."

"Duly noted." A confident, roguish grin spread across Alastor's face.

"Don't you smile at me like that," Melonie playfully scolded.

"Too late." Alastor kept his smile.

Melonie sighed dreamily. "Bria and I are about to go on recon and have to, you know, go dark and all that."

"Word. I'll just be out here, doing honest work cleaning up The Slums." Alastor looked around as he walked. "Holler if you need me. Better yet, hit me up with a code word."

Melonie giggled. "Like, *alpaca*?"

Alastor gasped. "That stays between you, me, and the sheets, you hear me?" he whispered.

"Relax, I haven't told anyone," Melonie said with a twisted smirk.

Alastor narrowed his eyes and groaned. "Just be safe, babe."

"Ok, I will. I—" Melonie's face suddenly went blank and she stopped talking.

"What was that?" Alastor asked, unwittingly. He had looked away while Melonie was talking to scratch the fuzz of his undercut.

"N— Nothing," Melonie stammered. "I'll let you know if we need help.

"Roger, roger." Alastor saluted Melonie with a confident smile as the call ended.

Alastor looked up. The shanty, shabbily built Slums towered over him. Soft rays of sunshine were the only remnants of the world beyond Downtown Slums. The sheet metal exteriors of the makeshift homes and shops were claustrophobic, and the narrow dirt road in front of him squeezed many of the impoverished citizens of the Slums close together. A few tired, weary, and hopeless citizens – Ski'tal and human alike – sat by the wayside, begging for the change of a more fortunate man.

Alastor spotted a small human child in ragged clothes; a Hispanic girl, probably no more than eight years old. She gave him a cutesy smile and waved. Her large, round eyes softened Alastor's heart and he smiled with something akin to fatherly warmth. "Hey kid," he knelt down to talk to her. "Where are your parents at?" he softly asked.

The girl shrugged. Alastor could hear the child's stomach growling. The girl looked down at her stomach, then back up at Alastor, not even reacting to the sound of her hunger. Alastor felt saddened and he stood up, patting his thighs before realizing that he didn't have pockets – but he felt his black MOLLE pack on his left hip. He unzipped it, pulled out a crisp Valhallan bill, and knelt back down. "Here's a clean twenty. Go nuts," he said as he handed the bill to the child. She gleefully grinned and hugged Alastor and he gently pat her on the back. "Get outta here, kid," he chuckled.

As the child ran off, Alastor spotted a cloaked figure standing at the edge of a nearby alleyway. Before his eyes could focus, the figure seemingly floated away. Alastor stared at the spot, but simply chose to ignore whatever it was he thought he saw.

"Shit," Alastor sighed. He stood up and cracked his lower back. "I could use a drink." Alastor looked over at a nearby bar, the harsh thumping and humming of the bass from the hip hop music playing inside calling to him like a siren out at sea.

Alastor pushed open the double doors and the harsh sunlight of The Slums was replaced by a dim, dank, sultry bar. A combination of humans and Ski'tal stood around the room, staring suspiciously at Alastor. He smiled daringly and walked towards the bar, humorously swaying his hips to the beat of the music. A grizzled, lanky man sat at a bar table, smoking a cigar. "This is my favorite song, Greg," Alastor leaned in and whispered to the man. Greg swiped at Alastor with a concealed knife, barely missing him. "Maybe next time!" Alastor called out. Greg folded his arms and mumbled to himself, deciding that pursuing Alastor wasn't worth his time. Alastor continued walking like nothing had happened.

He made it over to the bar and slid onto a bar stool, resting his elbows on the shabbily-made wooden counter. "*Privet*!" Alastor called out in Russian.

"You're getting good, friend!" A slim, white human bartender approached Alastor, drying a glass with a white towel speckled with holes. "Tough crowd, huh?" he said in a thick Russian accent.

Alastor sucked his teeth. "These guys are a bunch of lunatics," he said humorlessly. "But they ain't stupid. What's the special today, Vicktor?"

"Irish Trash Can," Vicktor said flatly.

"Vic, the Irish Trash Can is the special *every day."*

"Then why the hell did you ask?" Vicktor chuckled as he placed the clean glass back on the rack behind the bar.

Just as Alastor was about to respond, a massive knife swung down and slammed into the counter, narrowly missing him and sending splinters flying. Without much thought, Alastor grabbed the head of his assailant and slammed him face-first into the counter, immediately knocking him unconscious. Alastor raised his head up to see who it was.

"Steve?" Alastor said, shocked. "What the hell are you doing?" He sat Steve in the barstool next to him and quickly positioned him as though he were still in a conscious state of being.

"Remember when I said 'they ain't stupid'?" Alastor asked Vicktor as he nudged a nearby glass into Steve's limp hand. "Not this one. He ain't too bright."

"Doing God's work, I see." Vicktor slid a dark blue drink with a silver soda can submerged in the liquid into Alastor's hand.

"I'm telling you, Vicktor. When things get up and runnin' in here, we've gotta upgrade your arsenal." Alastor took a swig of the Trash Can and winced. "The fact that you don't have White Russians is a crime."

"Just because I'm Russian, I'm supposed to have White Russians?" Vicktor asked with a cheeky smile.

"Yes," Alastor said, smirking.

"So, it's okay with you if I stock up and make Black Russians?" Vicktor cracked a smile.

"Yes!" Alastor laughed heartily. He took another swig of the Trash Can. "Oh my God, that is rough," he quietly said to himself, choking down the sip.

As Alastor coughed, a hooded figure approached the bar and sat in the empty bar stool on the other side of him, plopping their arms down on the counter with a loud thud. Alastor had a look of mild confusion on his face as he tried to process why someone would bother him after making an example out of Steve. He turned his confused expression to Vicktor, who raised an eyebrow, showing that he was on the same page as Alastor.

Alastor looked on both sides of him, silently counting the empty bar stools before turning to the hooded figure. "Hey, uh... buddy. Don't mean to be that guy, but you got about seven to eight other options for seating that don't involve invading my personal space." Alastor sipped on his drink again as he glanced over at the front door. "I get it – free country and all that – but it's just a personal thing." He coughed again as he forced another sip down his throat.

Alastor took a closer look at the stranger. He saw navy blue armor plating on their hands and arms, and their fingers were interlocked in a poised manner; the armor was similar to his own. Alastor's heart pumped faster. He sat the drink down and placed his hand on the 1911 handgun on his right hip. "Is there something you wanna talk about, buddy?" Alastor adjusted his hand on his pistol several times to ensure he had a perfect purchase on the grip. "I'm not used to there being another armored guy 'round these parts, you feel me?"

"I feel you," a dark, female voice hummed under the hood. Alastor could practically hear the smile in her voice. His jaw slowly dropped and he tightened the grip on his pistol.

No...

"And I've waited *so long* to feel you." The hooded woman turned to face him. Alastor drew his pistol and aimed it directly at her before she could even reveal her face. Vicktor gasped and quickly backed away from them. The pounding music stopped abruptly. All the patrons in the bar quickly shot up to get a better look at what was happening.

Alastor's eyes frantically scanned over the woman. His brain couldn't process what he was experiencing and he started panting as if he had just finished a battle. His heart hadn't pounded this hard since he worked up the courage to talk to Melonie in The Vault. "Take off the hood." Alastor's hand trembled as he tried to keep the gun trained on the woman. His finger slipped onto the trigger and the woman chuckled as she pulled her hood off. A cloud of wavy brown hair billowed out from within. "Hello, Jack." A wide smirk spread across the human woman's slim brown face. Her pronounced, heart-shaped lips were two or three shades darker than her skin. She gazed into Alastor's eyes with her vibrant, electric blue irises; he felt like they were slicing into his soul.

Alastor seized up. In his head, he had pulled the trigger at least six times already, obliterating the shadow in front of him. But he couldn't move. He was paralyzed, a prisoner in his own body.

The woman placed two of her armored fingers on the barrel of Alastor's pistol and gently pushed it down and away from her. "Relax."

Alastor felt as though he had been splashed in the face with ice cold water. He jerked back, regaining control of himself and squeezed the trigger of his pistol, firing a round into the wooden floorboards of the bar. His 1911 flew out of his hand and clunked onto the floor. Alastor stepped back and grabbed the grip of his bastard sword on his left hip.

"Velanna," Alastor gasped.

"It's good to see you again, Alastor." Velanna stood up, but she appeared to be floating. Alastor silently stared at her, realizing that she was the cloaked shadow that had been tailing him in the streets.

"Jack," Velanna sang in a teasing voice, grinning with delight.

"Don't call me that," Alastor said defensively.

"He talks!" Velanna raised her hand to Alastor. "No need for all the hostility, my love." She walked past him, rubbing his bicep as she strolled by. "You look good. Gained some muscle?"

Alastor smacked her hand away. "Don't fucking touch me."

Unfazed, Velanna chuckled. She bent down and picked up Alastor's 1911. "There is something we need to discuss, my dear." She examined the age-old pistol, then looked up at Alastor. "My handler wishes to see you."

"Alright, Mel. Intel says the Legion is meetin' at Sinner's Circle, 10 klicks east." A tall, toned woman with almond skin racked the charging handle of her MP7 submachine gun. She wore a form-fitting set of black and yellow combat fatigues, adorned with an angular, abstract pattern. "You ready to head out?" she asked in a ruggedly feminine voice.

Melonie examined her dark purple armor for scratches and damage. The metal plating covered her chest, back, shoulders, and lower legs. The rest of her body was covered in a layer of Kevlar. "Uh, yeah, Bria," she stammered. Melonie rubbed the back of her neck and looked off into the distance. "Feels like I'm missing something..." But the sandy, uninhabited landscape before her did not jog her memory.

Bria knelt down and tied the laces of her combat boots. "The hell's gotten into you?"

"Nothing, I—" Melonie played with her hands. "I just have something on my mind."

Bria curled her pierced lip, trying to process what Melonie meant before speaking. "Right." She slung the strap of her submachine gun over her left shoulder and let it hang diagonally across her body. "C'mon. Gotta get goin'."

Bria walked alongside Melonie on the dirt path leading up a large hill. She scanned her eyes over Melonie, who wore a blank expression as she mindlessly walked alongside Bria, lost in her own little world.

What happened back there? Melonie thought. *I haven't felt that way before...*

Melonie studied her environment while she continued to process her thoughts. The Slums of Valhalla were the ruins of a Pre-Revolt Valhalla City. Even ten years later, the rusted remains of old 2000's-era vehicles remained in the streets of the abandoned city. The Slums were so big that one could traverse large areas without coming across a single soul for miles.

Melonie slowly turned her head to look at Bria, who was looking off into the distance. Her long, flowing black mane covered the entirety of her back and brushed the backs of her knees. "Bria?" Melonie finally spoke. Bria swung her head around to face Melonie, her brown eyes widening.

"I've been meaning to ask you," Melonie stuttered. "W— Why's your hair so long?"

Bria looked at Melonie like she had grown a second head. "It's like a second camouflage," Bria explained slowly. "Covers most of me when I crouch."

"Oh. Okay." Melonie looked back up at the path. She pretended to act like her question hadn't been awkward.

Bria's eyebrows furrowed. "Melonie." She stopped and placed a hand on her hip. "Was that really what you wanted to ask me?"

"...No?"

Bria groaned.

Alastor's heart pounded violently at the sight of Velanna. "Why should I trust you?"

Velanna chuckled as she played with the safety on Alastor's 1911. "What's not to trust about me, Jack?"

"Cut the shit." Alastor could barely look at Velanna. "Stop wasting my time."

"Fine, fine." Velanna moved back to her seat. "My handler hired me to retrieve one Alastor Hacon. Alive." She pressed the magazine release of the pistol, caught the falling magazine, observed how many rounds were left, and slapped it back into the gun. "He says it's something urgent – fate of Valhalla kind of thing." Velanna smirked at Alastor. "Isn't that *your* kind of gig anyways?" she spoke in a playful voice. She offered Alastor's gun back to him, flipping it around so the barrel pointed straight at her chest. Alastor saw a glimpse of what hid under Velanna's cloak – the armor did not stop at her arms. He snatched the pistol out of her hand.

"You should probably reload, by the way," she added as she leaned on the bar.

"Everything's just a game to you," Alastor hissed, holstering his 1911.

"Oh, yes, it is." Velanna checked the sharp, taloned nails of her armor. "And I play to win."

Melonie and Bria made their way up the dirt path that skirted the large mound. "What did you really want to ask me, Mel?" Bria asked.

Melonie's heart quickened and she felt butterflies in her stomach. A warm smile grew over her face before she could stop it. “Have you—” Melonie struggled to word her question. “When was the last time you fell for someone?”

“Fell? Why the hell would I fall down for someone?” Bria looked off into the distance. “I haven't fallen down since 2012,” she flatly stated.

“No, like... fell in love?”

Bria gulped. “I— Isn't there some kind of rule that says we can't talk about men or love or some shit like that?”

“What are you talking about? It's just a simple question.”

Bria turned pale. “It's... It's been a minute, not gonna lie.”

“Why, Bria?” Melonie asked softly.

“I gave up. Can’t say I didn’t try.” Bria refused to make eye contact with Melonie. “It’s kind of a weird topic.”

“Oh.” Melonie covered her mouth. “Bria, I'm sorry, I didn't mean—”

“No, you're fine.” Bria wrapped her arms around herself as she shivered. “My dad always told me about how mom was ‘the one’. His soulmate.” Bria squeezed herself even tighter to control her body as the shivering intensified but, still, she smiled. “He said she had a smile that could melt the iceberg that sunk the Titanic – or somethin' like that.”

Melonie faintly smiled.

"Then one day, the doctors said my mom had lung cancer. Gave her six months. I used that time to prepare myself for the day, y'know?" Melonie glanced at Bria, who looked both hurt and at peace. "She looked good for a lady in her last days." Bria paused. Melonie watched as she smiled to herself, but it faded away as fast as it had appeared. "She died one day, outta nowhere. Four months early." Bria looked down at the path she was walking. "Went in her sleep."

"Oh, Bria…" Melonie sighed empathetically.

"Dad's been alone since. And I ain't got the balls to go check on him."

Melonie looked at Bria with concern. "Well, maybe your mother's looking down on you too." A small smile spread across Melonie's face. "Pretty sure she's proud of you, B."

"Yeah, maybe." Bria smiled softly. "C'mon. We're almost there."

Bria and Melonie reached the top of the mound, which was actually a massive crater. At the base of the crater was a sea of Ski'tal, and a metal stage was positioned at the front of the crowd. Bria looked to her left and pointed to an unfinished building. "There. That's a good vantage point."

Bria and Melonie crouched down and made their way to the unfinished concrete building. They both climbed to the top platform and lay prone. "Do you have the binoculars?" Melonie asked.

"Oh shit. I— I thought you had them," Bria stammered.

Melonie stared at Bria, slack-jawed. Bria snickered as she pulled the binoculars from her hip bag and handed them to Melonie. She sighed. "You and Alastor hang out too much." Melonie placed the binoculars up to her face and scanned the stage.

On the stage, a large, metal being stood in a domineering stance. "Your support for the Legion is comforting," he said to the audience, his mohawk of vibrant synthetic red hair flowing in the breeze. His vocoded, flanged voice was loud enough that Melonie and Bria could hear him clearly.

"Target confirmed," Melonie whispered.

"Ryze got some new duds," Bria whispered to herself.

Ryze pointed into the audience with his large, clawed hand. "Since The Vault Incident, our numbers have grown nearly twofold – an unexpected boon to our cause." He placed his hand on his large, metal-plated chest. "For that, I am grateful." Ryze paced across the stage. The regal, scarlet waistcloth attached to his metal hips trailed behind him.

"That doesn't sound good," Bria whispered to Melonie. She gave Bria a concerned look and wearily turned her gaze back to the binoculars.

"Last year, our people suffered a great loss when our great Vinton Degon was assassinated in this very spot," Ryze continued. His emerald green eyes scanned the crowd from beneath a pair of large red plates that served as his eyebrows. "And Fel, my queen, was killed later that year at the hands of Alastor Hacon, leader of Blur Havok." The crowd of Ski'tal nodded their heads in respect. "You all have been supportive of me in my time of grief, and I am grateful for that."

"Someone took a chill pill…" Melonie muttered.

"Yeah, I'm used to more yellin' than this," Bria concurred.

"Our next course of action will be swift and decisive. We will be ready to strike at the heart of New Valhalla City in a matter of days," Ryze said, returning to his authoritative tone. "The war will end in *our* favor." The crowd erupted into a joyous applause.

Bria patted Melonie on the shoulder. "How much more intel we need?"

"There's one last thing..." Melonie drawled.

Ryze raised his hand and the crowd quickly quieted themselves. "I know you are concerned about one *certain* thing." He placed his hands behind his tapered waist. "Rest assured, our people's greatest secret remains uncompromised. And it will remain that way..." A smile grew on Ryze's steel-plated face, "...Melonie Sanders."

Melonie gasped and looked at Bria, who was already reaching for Melonie.

"In the very spot where Leah, the human agent, killed our Vinton, lies two Blur Havok officers," Ryze calmly informed the mob of Ski'tal. "Apprehend them for me, please." He swatted at the crowd in a dismissive fashion. "I will join you shortly."

An unholy choir of metallic war cries and screams called out for the blood of both women as the crowd of Ski'tal clamored to chase after Melonie and Bria. They hastily ran down the hill they had traversed, slipping several times on the gravel. "Now would be a good time for EVAC!" Melonie told Bria.

Bria raised her wrist. "Ozzi, Mason, do either of you copy?" Gunfire erupted from behind them. "Shit!" Bullets hit the ground near the duo's feet. "Code red! We need help ASAP!"

An Australian male's voice responded. "Roger. ETA is 20 mikes."

"That is way too long. I've got a plan B." Melonie raised her wrist.

“C'mon, Alastor.” Velanna traced her finger around the lip of Alastor's drink. “I know you want to end this war.” She plucked the empty silver can out of the drink and flicked it at Vicktor, who flinched. “I'm giving you an out here.”

“This has got to be a joke.” Alastor narrowed his eyes and scrunched up his face. “Did you forget what you did?”

“Jog my memory, Jack.” Velanna poked her temple. “It's a little fuzzy.”

Alastor stepped up to Velanna. “How about I show you?”

Velanna bit her lip as she looked at Alastor.

“If I catch you within eyesight of me or The Bureau, I will tear your chest open with my bare hands.” Alastor's wrist vibrated loudly, followed by a series of beeps.

“Sounds like the missus is calling.” Velanna pointed at Alastor's arm.

Alastor backed away from Velanna and answered the call. “Yeah, babe?”

Melonie was panting loudly. The sound of gunfire almost stifled her cry for help. “Alpaca! Alpaca!” she screamed.

"Send me your location." Alastor turned towards the exit of the bar. "I'm on my way." Alastor ended the call. "Sorry about the floor, Vicktor."

"Still using that safe word, I see?" Velanna giggled.

Alastor's face twisted up in disgust. "Stay away or I'll kill you." Alastor stomped towards the exit.

"I look forward to it."

"Get fucked." Alastor barged out of the double doors and into the harsh sunlight.

Chapter 2

"Quick, that way!" Bria pointed towards the abandoned houses. The duo ran down the destroyed streets of Old Valhalla City as a wave of Ski'tal pressed on after them, firing their guns at the duo. "Where's your Plan B, Mel?" Bria yelled.

"Give him a few seconds!" Melonie responded.

"You know what they say about seconds countin', right?" Bria raised her MP7 behind her and let loose a spray of bullets to fend off the troops.

"What's that?"

"'Help is only minutes away'!"

Melonie groaned. "Not helping!" She fired her UMP submachine gun behind them, cutting down a few drones, only to be quickly replaced by more.

"Melonie," Bria anxiously called out. "We're runnin' out of road here!" A large pile of rubble and collapsed buildings walled off any accessible portion of the path ahead. The two slowed their pace to a halt as they looked at the insurmountable debris. They both turned around to see that the drones had slowed down too and were aiming their weapons at them.

Ryze floated ominously above them with his triangular wings deployed upwards, his arms clasped regally behind his back. Melonie fired her UMP at Ryze's chest but the bullets deflected off his chest and ricocheted into the ground. “Crap,” Melonie muttered.

“Lessons were learned, small one. Now, I have to ask,” Ryze smiled, “what are two high ranking Blur Havok members doing all the way out here?”

“News flash, dickhead,” Bria barked. “We're still in a Civil War.”

“And we just found out your next move,” Melonie said, pointing at Ryze.

“Then you heard me clearly when I said our forces have only grown since your attempt at genocide.” Ryze's face darkened. “You can't possibly hope to defeat us.”

The sound of an energized growl echoed in the air and a blue cloud of energy formed right in front of Bria and Melonie. From the haze, Alastor rose up with a grin on his face, sword in hand. “Now we can.” Alastor flicked his left forearm and a large, silver shield extended from the center. “The fight just got fair.”

Ryze growled under his breath. “Beat them into the ground,” he ordered as he pointed at the trio. “Bring me their broken bodies.”

A battle mask covered Alastor's face from his chin to his nose. “Just like old times, buddy-boy!” he yelled as he slammed his sword against his shield. The drones charged at Alastor, firing their guns at him. He raised his shield to cover his face and the bullets ricocheted off of it. As the troops reached Alastor, he swatted his shield at the vanguards of the crowd, sending several Ski'tal flying.

"Alastor!" Melonie yipped happily. "You're actually using the shield!" She fired at the drones flanking Alastor.

"What," Alastor pulled a SCAR assault rifle off of his back and shielded himself from gunfire, "you thought I was lying?" He fired his rifle in bursts as he backed away, dropping drones in sets of twos and threes. "This is the best birthday gift ever!"

Bria scoffed as she fired from behind a nearby car. "Says the guy who pretended to have amnesia and forget his girlfriend's first kiss."

"Comedy is a fine art that will not be appreciated by everyone." Alastor drove the bottom of his shield into the cracked street. He detached it from his arm, grabbed a drone by the head, and smashed her face into the horned top of the shield, impaling her. Alastor dove behind the shield and effortlessly reattached it to his forearm. He swung it around and tossed the corpse at the mob of Ski'tal. They all tumbled to the ground.

"How quaint." Ryze dove down and grabbed Alastor by his shield, yanking him closer. "You have new toys." He was a hulking, towering metal terror compared to Alastor. His head barely reached Ryze's reinforced chest.

Alastor struggled to break Ryze's grip on his shield, but he held on effortlessly. A series of large metal panels slid into place to cover the entirety of Ryze's face. Alastor slammed his rifle down on his head, but Ryze simply tilted his head and chuckled. "You're not the only one who's upgraded." Ryze grabbed Alastor's neck and flung him through the air. He landed on his back with a loud *crunch* as his armor smashed the black asphalt underneath him. Ryze used his wings to launch into the air with a powerful burst. One of his wrist-mounted blades shot out and Alastor rolled out of the way as Ryze landed with a loud *thud*, his blade puncturing the ground beneath him.

Alastor gasped as he tried to regain his breath, but a drone kicked him in the face before he could get his bearings. Alastor swatted the insect-like drone into the air with his shield and fired his rifle, sending a bullet through his chest. Yellow blood poured from the sky as Ski'tal parts rained down. Alastor returned the rifle to his back. and unsheathed his sword. "Melonie," Alastor called out. "Hate to be negative, but this ain't my most effective fighting style."

Bria caught wind of Alastor's struggle. "Melonie, focus your fire on Ryze. I'm on crowd control."

Melonie nodded as she leaned out of cover and took several careful shots at Ryze. Cyan blood spurted from the synthetic muscle of his bicep and he glared at Melonie from behind his battle mask. Even though his eyes were hidden, Melonie could tell that Ryze had his sights set on her. He ripped his knife out of the asphalt and transformed his hand into a belt-fed machine gun. Melonie scurried behind a large pile of debris and ducked down as bullets perforated the wreckage.

Alastor watched in horror as Melonie fled from Ryze but before he could act, more drones assaulted him.

They clawed and swung relentlessly at Alastor, but he kept them at bay with his shield. Alastor growled angrily. "You shitheads didn't learn the first time." He saw Ryze reload his machine gun, giving Melonie a moment of reprieve. Alastor warped out of the drones' grasp and the horde collapsed on top of one another. When they managed to stand back up, they found that he had vanished.

Alastor suddenly reappeared and sliced through a wave of drones, disemboweling them. They fell to the ground, holding their intestines. Alastor dug his fingers into the chest of a drone and ripped the drone completely in half. He walked through the slaughtered drone and drew his pistol. His bullets burst the heads of several Ski'tal as he continued making his way towards Ryze. Alastor viciously slammed his sword deep into the head of a charging drone, who gargled on his own blood. He ripped his sword from the drone's head and hurled it at Ryze. He had just finished reloading his machine gun when Alastor's sword pierced right through it. He screamed out, clutching his damaged arm. Alastor warped to Ryze and grabbed the hilt of the sword.

"She's not the one to fuck with," Alastor hissed.

He yanked the sword upwards, filleting Ryze's arm. Alastor kicked Ryze away from him, knocking him off balance. Ryze looked at his damaged forearm, frayed and missing the mechanical bone that held it together. His battle mask retracted and a twisted, angry expression appeared from within. His eyes turned blood red. "Suffocate them," he commanded his troops.

Alastor warped to Melonie. He grabbed her by the shoulders and moved her behind an abandoned house. Alastor detached his shield and placed it on his back, over the rifle. "You ok, babe?" He held Melonie's hand and checked her body for signs of damage or injury.

"Yeah, I'm fine. Are you?"

Alastor chuckled. "You know how I get when my girl's in trouble," he said. Melonie smiled as bullets grazed and bounced off of Alastor's shield.

"Alastor!" Melonie gasped. She placed her hand on Alastor's bicep. The Kevlar on his arm was ripped and a bullet wound was under the torn fabric. "You're hurt!"

"Pistol round. It looks like it went clean through." Alastor shrugged. "I'll be fine."

"Wait." Melonie placed her hand on Alastor's chest and an LED menu with three icons appeared: a power symbol, a question mark, and an exclamation point. Melonie delicately pressed the exclamation point.

"Bullet wound located." Alastor's armor said in a female voice. "Cauterizing."

A soft hissing sound came from Alastor's bicep. He winced and he sucked in air through his teeth as the blood stopped leaking from his arm. "Thanks, babe," Alastor softly said. Melonie placed her hand on Alastor's face.

"Hey guys," Bria slid into cover next to them. "I know, third wheelin' and cock blockin' seems to be my thing, but we can't stay here any longer. This is almost triple what Ryze hit us with at Keine a few months back."

"I can help," a female voice said. Alastor whipped around. His heart stopped and his blood froze.

"Holy fuck..." Bria muttered as she looked behind Alastor.

"Velanna Brandie, at your service." She placed a hand on her hip.

"Uh..." Melonie looked at both Bria and Alastor. "Who is this?"

Velanna walked past Alastor, brushing her armored hand over his shoulder. "C'mon. Can't hold them off if you're hiding, Jack." Bria looked at Alastor with a dead expression.

"Hell..." Alastor muttered to himself. "We're holding the line," he told Bria and Melonie.

"This is gonna suck." Bria reloaded her MP7, then followed Velanna into the battlefield.

"You're telling me," Alastor grunted before he warped away. Melonie looked dumbfounded as she tried to process what was happening.

Alastor warped above Velanna, firing his rifle into the crowd. He landed on a drone and pulled out his shield. Alastor hid behind it as he fired his rifle into the wave of Ski'tal. Bria ran up behind him and placed her hand on his shoulder. They nodded and Bria covered Alastor's back, firing at any drones who tried to flank him.

"You're better than I thought, Jack!" Velanna called out to Alastor. He groaned loudly over the bedlam underneath him. She chuckled and stripped off her brown cloak, revealing her sleek, navy blue armor. It was modeled similarly to Alastor's, covering her chest, hips, legs, and back. She even had a dark green cloth attached to her waist. Velanna pulled a short barrel shotgun from the small of her back and fired several slugs into drone after drone, their bodies splitting open in gnarled ribbons of synthetic gore. Each shot was followed by the vicious crack of Velanna pumping the action of the shotgun, ejecting a smoldering empty shell.

Melonie joined the fight and pulled out her P226 pistol. She fired at two drones charging Velanna, dropping them instantly. Velanna stood aloof from Melonie and turned up her nose. Melonie, who was oblivious to Velanna's disdain, ran over to Bria and Alastor.

"Anyone hit?" Melonie asked the pair.

"Nah, I'm good," Bria said.

"You know what's up," Alastor grinned.

Despite his lighthearted attitude, Alastor remained focused as the onslaught continued. "Nigga, what the fuck?" Bria called out. Alastor looked back at Velanna and saw three drones collapse in sequence in front of her. They all had clean, gargantuan-sized holes in different parts of their bodies. Velanna winked when she noticed Alastor looking at her and blew him a kiss.

Alastor turned back around and grumbled under his breath. "Jesus Christ." Alastor turned to Melonie. "What's the ETA on EVAC?" he yelled.

"Should be here any minute now!" Melonie answered.

"What did I say about minutes earlier?" Bria smirked as she pulled the pin on a grenade and tossed it.

"Bria, shut it," Melonie hissed. She threw one of her daggers into the head of a drone. The explosion of Bria's grenade kicked up a considerable amount of dust. Velanna stood just beyond the cloud and three more Ski'tal with massive holes lay at her feet. Melonie caught her eye as Velanna brushed herself off. She smirked at Melonie before dashing into the battle, her long, dark green cloak trailing behind her like a serpent's tail.

"Something or other, seconds away?" Alastor asked. He swapped to his 1911 when his SCAR ran dry.

Bria sucked her teeth. "And people say I'm uncultured," she said in a posh accent. "Absolute degenerates."

"Wow," Alastor drawled. "Someone knows her SAT words."

"Eh," Bria unsheathed her knife and stabbed a drone in the head before ripping it off at the base of the skull. "Hang out with Ozzi for a few weeks and you end up soundin' like a politician."

A drone shot Bria in the leg, creating a bloodless wound. Bria grunted loudly and raised her gun to fire. Before she could retaliate, the drone's upper half exploded, sending purple blood and synthetic body parts everywhere. Velanna emerged from behind the dead Ski'tal and lightly pushed him over with her smoking shotgun. "You're welcome," Velanna smirked. Bria spitefully sneered at Velanna.

Ryze floated above the Legion. "The Slums' most shameful criminal," he said pointing at Velanna. "Stand down before you are put down like the dog you are."

Velanna crushed the throat of a drone. "I have business with them." She shook the gore off of her hand as the drone's body fell to the ground. "And there's no shame in what I do," she said, grinning.

Velanna ran at the horde of drones and Alastor watched her disappear in front of him from behind his shield. Several drones collapsed onto the ground in a heap of parts, dispersing a large portion in front of the Blur Havok team.

"Did someone call for help?" a male voice said over Melonie's comms.

A large gunship flew from behind Sinner's Circle and quickly approached the battle. Ryze immediately noticed and gasped. "Retreat!" he yelled to his troops.

The company of Ski'tal began to flee as the gunship hovered above the Legion. A ramp opened on the bottom of the ship and an albino man in large, bulky green and black armor stood at the bottom with a Minigun. "Heavy ordinance!" the man yelled excitedly. The multiple barrels on the Minigun began spinning and sprayed thousands of bullets at the Legion and several drones exploded in the hail of lead. Ryze's mask quickly formed just as a bullet struck him in the center of his face. He careened backward as he tried to flee. The armored gunner didn't stop until the Ski'tal had completely disappeared. The team rose from behind Alastor's shield, surveying the carnage. They all let out a collective sigh.

"Woo!" Velanna exclaimed, approaching the group. "That was pretty fun!"

"You guys wanna talk about what her deal is?" Melonie quietly asked. "A friend, maybe?"

Alastor shook his head. "Not even close." He folded his arms, Bria placed her hand on her hips, and Melonie kept glancing at the two trying to figure out why everyone, *except her*, knew each other.

"Great job! Put 'er there!" Velanna held out her hand, offering a handshake. Alastor looked at the gesture like it was an insult, then slowly moved his unimpressed eyes up to match Velanna's.

"No? Okay!" Velanna offered her hand to Bria, only for Bria to immediately slap Velanna's hand away from her.

"Fuck off," Bria growled.

"Fine by me." Velanna smiled as she moved to Melonie, only to pull her hand away from her, curling her fingers and bringing her hand close to her chest. "You'll be fine," Velanna said flatly. Melonie raised her eyebrows in shock at the audacity of Velanna.

The gunship lowered from the sky and its large propellers blew swaths of dust at the group as it landed with a heavy thud. "Sorry, fashionably late again," the albino man said in a deep, nasally voice as he pulled off his goggles and sat them on top of his flowing blonde locks. His face suddenly turned sour when he spotted Velanna. "What the bloody hell is she doing here?"

"Not surprised you know her, Ozzi," Alastor said.

"How could I forget the witch who ran off with my first armor prototype?" Ozzi stepped off the gunship. "Let's kick rocks before she follows us home."

"Okay, wait!" Melonie threw up her hands. "Wait." She slowly lowered her hands and calmed down. "Can someone explain what's going on here and who this woman is?"

"Velanna Brandie," Alastor sighed. "Deadly criminal, gun-for-hire..."

"Thief..." Ozzi added.

"Mega assaholic bitch," Bria stacked on top.

"And Alastor's *previous girlfriend.* " Velanna directed her smile at Melonie, waiting to feed off of her reaction – she was not disappointed.

Melonie felt a sharp stab in her heart as those words left Velanna's lips. She immediately looked at Alastor, perturbed. He covered his face with his armored claws and let out an embarrassed groan.

"Well, you *did* ask..." Velanna teased Melonie.

"Why are you here?" Bria pointed at Velanna. "Hurry up, before I do something I *won't* regret."

"Bria's proclivity for violence seems quite applicable here," Ozzi said.

"I'm glad civility is still appreciated, even in these insane times." Velanna placed her hands behind her back. "As I told Alastor before, my handler has requested his presence at his domicile. Dare I say, the fate of Valhalla lies in Alastor's cooperation."

"Man," Bria sucked her teeth. "This sounds sketch as hell."

"You said it yourself. That attack was nearly three times the size of the attack on your outpost two months ago, correct?"

"Ryze himself confirmed that," Melonie sheepishly said.

Alastor looked intensely at Melonie, only because he was trying to keep his composure. She looked back at him with large, doleful eyes. Alastor turned to Velanna, arms still folded. "Alright, where's your handler?"

"I have to take you to him. His identity is information that is *need-to-know*," Velanna said, maintaining her unbothered, playful expression.

"Nuh-uh. He's not going alone," Ozzi spoke up.

"Yeah, I don't like this." Melonie tensed up, furrowing her eyebrows.

"Not possible." Velanna frowned for the first time since her debut. "'No guests, for the moment.' His words exactly."

Alastor groaned. "Fine, whatever. Take me to the son of a bitch." He faced the rest of his team. "Head back to The Bureau and await further orders."

A grin slowly spread across Velanna's face. "Finally, he accepts the call to action."

Alastor looked at Melonie, who had a look that would make a weaker man give her everything he owned. Alastor approached her. The armor around his hand retracted and exposed a gloved hand. Alastor cupped her soft cheek. "It'll be fine, babe," he said softly, the bass in his voice warming Melonie's heart. He leaned down and kissed her lips. "Trust me."

Melonie couldn't help but smile. "Okay. Be safe."

Alastor nodded and walked away from Melonie, following Velanna. He punched towards the ground to extend the armor around his hand. Alastor paused and turned back to Ozzi. "For future reference, it's *ordnance*, not ordinance." He pointed at Ozzi with a sly smile.

Ozzi chuckled. "I was waiting for one of you guys to catch it."

"Come now, it's not far." Velanna turned her back on the team. Alastor slowly followed.

Melonie and the rest of the team reluctantly boarded the gunship without Alastor. "Mason, get us outta here," Bria said. Melonie dropped into a seat as the gunship lifted into the sky. She lowered her head into her hands and began to lose herself in her thoughts, feeling a familiar kind of darkness encroaching on her mind.

Bria looked at Melonie's pitiful state. "Hey, hey, hey!" she barked. "I know that look. Get out of your head."

"I can't help it, Bria!" Melonie's voice raised in pitch. "What am I supposed to do when my boyfriend is out there with an ex I just met?"

Bria stared at Melonie for a few seconds. The rattling of the overhead straps and hooks kept it from being completely silent. "Wow," she whispered. "He really hasn't told you anythin' about this girl, has he?" Melonie shook her head.

Bria sat next to her. "Mel, trust me. The fact that she's even alive is some kind of screwed up miracle." Bria placed her hand on Melonie's back. "If Alastor smells somethin' fishy, there won't be anything left of that bitch." Bria leaned back in her seat and placed her hands on her legs. "Besides, with a rap sheet like hers, I wouldn't tell any girlfriend of mine that I dated her either.

Melonie sighed and forced a smile onto her face. "You're right," she muttered. "You know better than I do."

"You're damn right I do," Bria said smugly. "Now relax. I have a feeling it's 'bout to be a long day."

Chapter 3

"You make me feel amazing, Jack," Velanna sweetly said.

"I'm glad I do," Alastor murmured in her ear, his arm wrapped around her waist. He softly pecked the base of Velanna's bare neck. The two lay under the covers in bed, skin-to-skin.

"You know, I've been thinking..." Velanna said in a higher pitch than normal. Alastor's hand rested on her naked abdomen and she sensually ran her fingers over it. "You don't *have* to go back to Blur Havok, right?"

"Of course not," Alastor purred. "They don't need me."

"I've been thinking of giving up this life." Velanna rolled over and faced Alastor. "It's only fair, right?"

"Yeah." Alastor looked at Velanna's soft, heart-shaped lips. "You know how I feel about that stuff."

"I've been a good girl," Velanna pouted.

"Have you?" Alastor chuckled. "Didn't seem like you were just now."

"You and that sense of humor," Velanna scoffed.

"I was told only the funny guys get the girls."

"How do you even know it works?" Velanna fluttered her eyelashes.

"Seems to be working so far." Alastor leaned in close to Velanna and kissed her passionately. She placed her hand on his neck and kissed him back.

"Jack..."

Alastor did not respond.

"Jack?"

Alastor shook his head and grunted, realizing that Velanna was speaking to him. "Don't call me that."

Alastor held his 1911 in his hand as he and Velanna walked through The Slums.

"What?" Velanna smiled. "You looked like you were daydreaming." She placed her finger on her lip. "Or maybe you were remembering something...?"

"Shut the fuck up." Alastor continued to follow Velanna. "How much farther?"

"Not far," Velanna said. "My handler likes to live away from the riff-raff."

Velanna slipped past a group of Ski'tal. Alastor placed his hand on one that was in his way and the Ski'tal scowled at him, but upon further inspection, he didn't see the value in intimidating a soldier that was armed to the teeth. He turned back around and wisely minded his own business.

"So, I've been keeping up with your antics, Jack," Velanna playfully said. Velanna swayed her wide hips side to side as she walked. She slyly looked at Alastor behind her as she strolled forward.

Alastor silently scanned his environment, ignoring her.

"The Vault was pretty nuts, huh?"

Alastor press checked his pistol. There was a silver hollow-point round in the chamber. He continued to ignore Velanna.

"Oh, c'mon Jack. There's no need to be so aloof. Think of it as a little family reunion."

Alastor holstered his 1911 and swung his SCAR rifle off of his back. He swapped out the used magazine for a full one with thirty rounds in it. He silently swung it back over his shoulder and drew his 1911 again.

"That pistol looks kinda familiar–"

"Do you ever shut up?" Alastor finally snapped at Velanna. "It's like you're purposefully *trying* to annoy me."

Velanna gasped. "I never!" She placed her hand on her chest dramatically. "Did all those months we dated count for nothing? Not even a 'good to see you'?" She smiled, breaking the facade. “It’s okay, Jack. I know you valued our time like I did.”

“I thank God every day that it’s over,” Alastor mumbled.

Velanna and Alastor made their way to a lone shack in the middle of a large empty area. The only things that surrounded the shack were puddles of mucky water and small plots of muddy ground. It was only big enough for two people to stand comfortably inside. “What, is your handler taking a shit in here or something?” Alastor groaned impatiently.

“There's always more than meets the eye, Alastor.” Velanna opened the door to the shack. A glossy black elevator awaited inside.

Alastor's heart sped up. “Velanna, I swear to God...” he said wearily.

“It's okay,” Velanna giggled. “He wants you *alive,* silly.” The doors to the elevator slid open and its carbon-fiber interior awaited – there was only one button. The two stood side-by-side as the elevator descended. The ride was so smooth that Alastor wondered if the elevator was even moving; it wasn’t until he felt a slight jostle of the elevator car that he was certain.

Alastor holstered his 1911, but kept his hand on it. Velanna lifted her hand into the air. “Velanna, you touch me again, and I'll cut off your hand.”

Velanna groaned. "God, Alastor, I was just going to fix my hair."

"Can't trust you any farther than I can throw you."

"Such a shame," Velanna sighed, fluffing her wavy brown hair. "If my memory serves correctly, you're a pretty good thrower," she said provocatively.

Alastor sighed. He shifted in his armor, trying his hardest to ignore the night that Velanna was referring to. Suddenly, the doors slid open and a glossy black room with a tall, leering atrium greeted them. A long strip of white carbon fiber formed a path to a lone chair at the end of the room. A fireplace sat in front of the chair, and a warm, orange fire roared inside of it.

Alastor squinted until his eyes adjusted to the dark room, revealing a man sitting in the shadow of the fire. A digitigrade leg was crossed over the other and his elbows rested on the armrests of the chair, his fingers steepled in front of his face. "Knights," the man said in a cold and commanding voice. He turned his head and his dreadlocks swayed through the air. "Come to me."

"No way..." Alastor raised his eyebrows. He drew his pistol, but as soon as the gun left his holster, Alastor felt a wave of static electricity wash over his arms and legs and he felt pins and needles throughout his limbs, as if they had fallen asleep. The 1911 dropped out of his hand. Alastor caught a glimpse of the man holding his hand up to him before he fell limply to the ground.

"Iskander," the man called out. "Assist him, please."

A towering man strode sternly over to Alastor's limp body. He grabbed him by his back with a steel-clawed hand and lifted him up to eye level. He was olive-skinned, with a bearded face and vibrant red eyes that scanned Alastor judgmentally before holding him up for the man in the shadows to see.

"There's no way..." Alastor repeated in shock.

"Now, now..." the man slowly rose from his seat, showing his age. "There's no need for that." He walked towards Alastor's immobilized body. A trio of silhouettes emerged from behind the cloaked man and approached him as well. Alastor drooped awkwardly from Iskander's grasp. The only part of his body he was able to move was his face.

The human man stepped into the light, revealing a brown, bearded face and frosted dreadlocks. His body was wrapped in sleek black and blood-red armor with twisted pieces of metal accenting his shoulders, forearms, chest, and thighs. He had a sharp, angular headpiece that resembled a pair of horns. "Hello, Alastor." His voice was weathered, chilling, and brought back many long-lost emotions.

Alastor began to visibly brew with anger. "I knew it! You son of a bitch!" he shouted, tears forming in his eyes. "Who the hell do you think you are?"

"That's no way to speak to your father," the man said with a smile. He turned to Velanna. "Well done."

"Wasn't too hard, Roark." Velanna grinned as she watched Alastor dangle helplessly in front of them.

"It's been ages, son." Roark patted Alastor's face with his unskinned synthetic hand. He scanned his son as though he could see the changes Alastor's body had undergone. "You've definitely installed quite a few synthetic implants." Roark's eye twitched as he looked at Alastor's chest. "Alleviating your asthma with them as well? It definitely has been far too long."

"Who's fuckin' fault is that?" Alastor screamed. "You deadbeat bastard! You abandoned us."

"I did not take my leave from you and your mother lightly," Roark said, frowning. "I had a calling that needed to be answered."

"Why did you leave me?" Alastor cried out.

Roark looked visibly taken aback. "I– I didn't leave you. I left your *mother*. If I'd had it my way, I would've taken you with me."

"First Velanna, now this bullshit," Alastor hissed. "What'd you get her involved for?"

"I figured you'd react to my presence this way," Roark said. "I needed her to bring you here under ambiguous pretenses, because otherwise..."

"You knew I'd tell you to kick rocks," Alastor said evenly. "But, for the record, Velanna is not a better alternative."

"I needed someone who would catch your eye. Someone you have a history with."

Alastor glared at his father. "At least you know something about me. Or you did your research."

Roark tilted his head. "Alastor, I know our pasts are sordid, but what matters is that we're here now, together," Roark said, observing his son. Alastor stared at Roark.

"I missed you, my son."

A single tear fell down Alastor's cheek and a hesitant smile broke through. "I missed you too, dad," he said, his voice breaking.

Roark nodded to Iskander. As soon as Iskander dropped Alastor, feeling was restored to his limbs. Alastor stumbled when he landed, but he quickly regained his balance. "Um, thanks," he said, wiping his face clean.

"My plans are finally coming to fruition," Roark sighed in relief. "All of my children, together at last."

Alastor narrowed his eyes. "Children? Plural?"

"Meet your siblings." Roark grinned. "The Knights of Hacon." From the shadows stepped three battle-ready warriors: two men and one woman.

The woman quickly approached Alastor, walking on synthetic appendages that lacked any articulation from the knee down – just sharp, pointed tips that she was somehow able to balance effortlessly on. She wore a short, indigo robe that hugged her figure and a pair of compression shorts covered her thighs under her neatly segmented robe. Her hands were lacking synthetic skin, instead showing the full wiring of her synthetic muscles. She leaned in closely to get a better look at Alastor, and he noticed that her dark-skinned face was decorated with tribal tattoos. The woman examined him with orange, cat-like eyes. "Brother? Interesting," she muttered, her voice hissing like a snake.

"Okay. Personal space, please." Alastor backed away. "This girl is my sister?"

"Yes." Roark glowed at the sight of seeing his children meet for the first time.

"Sreda is my name," she said. Sreda grinned widely and a full set of grey synthetic teeth gleamed from her mouth. Her smile was wild, but well-meaning.

Alastor did a double-take. "Wait, what? How do you spell that?"

Sreda awkwardly obliged, scratching her wild, dark blue hair. "S-R-E-D-A"

"Wow." Alastor stroked his beard. "And, uh, how exactly is that pronounced?"

"Ez-red-uh?" Sreda said as she raised an eyebrow.

"Are you making this up?"

"No..." Sreda said, folding her arms across her chest.

Alastor looked back and forth at Roark and Sreda with a bewildered expression. "Dad, what the fuck happened here?"

Roark's eyebrows sank. "Alastor..."

"Well, he doesn't seem too bad to me." An Afro-Asian man in black and yellow armor approached. His black, wavy hair was in a short ponytail. His armor was moderate, like Alastor's, and he had plating on his chest, back, shoulders, and shins. A short, black coattail trailed behind him. His snarky, raucous voice matched the swagger of his walk. His height, however, did not; he was nearly four inches shorter than Alastor. "Sreda's weird, don't sweat it."

"Your innards are fuck, Arashi," Sreda cursed.

Arashi's face contorted into a disgruntled expression. The look had a million stories behind it. "See?" he said to Alastor.

"Wait a minute," Alastor said. "What's wrong with—?"

"Hi, I'm Malachi." A young, fair-skinned teen walked up to Alastor, offering his gloved hand and a glowing white grin. He was clearly the youngest – his round head, youthful eyes, scarce facial hair, and close-cropped hair screamed naïve. Although he wore no armor, his long, flowing black and green tunic was clearly designed by the same person that designed the armor for the other Knights. "I've seen so much of your work." The bright, energetic sound of Malachi's voice was almost painful to Alastor's ears.

Alastor accepted Malachi's hand and shook it slowly. "Hi, Malachi." Alastor looked around and spotted Velanna giggling at Alastor's obvious discomfort. He quickly averted his eyes. "Shit's gettin' weird, man..." Alastor muttered to himself. He was starting to feel a little overwhelmed with the nature of the situation.

"Yep, sounds like a regular ole' Wednesday around here," Arashi said.

There was one introduction that had not been made yet. Alastor turned to Iskander. "So... what about you?" Alastor said.

"You already know my name," Iskander said in a booming voice. He glared down at him and his red eyes were just like Alastor's. He was a hulking armored rock, covered from head to toe in metal plates. His large chest was adorned with a black and orange stole that draped down to his thighs.

"Yeah, Iskander. But don't you have some kinda schtick?" Alastor said, trying to defuse the tension. "Some kind of sparkling personality trait?"

"No. There is no time for games." Iskander walked past Alastor, his armor plates clanking together. Each step of his steel-toe boots could be felt across the room. “Time is of the essence.”

“What's André the Giant talking about?” Alastor asked Roark.

“Inaccurate. Iskander is only six-foot, two—” Sreda began matter-of-factly.

“Not now, Sreda,” Iskander said in the distance.

“He's right. Everyone, to the briefing room,” Roark said strictly, following Iskander.

Alastor turned to Velanna as the rest of the Knights fell in line. “No seriously, what is up with her?”

“Thanks for the ride, Mason,” Bria said as she waved to the gunship’s pilot.

“Don't mention it, ma’am,” Mason said, flipping switches to power down the ship. “Drinks are on you, though.” His bearded, Caucasian face smirked from the cockpit.

Bria, Melonie, and Ozzi stepped off the gunship. “I'm ready to take this armor off. It’s starting to chafe,” Ozzi groaned.

“I need a bubble bath and a foot massage,” Bria said, walking alongside Ozzi. “Also, baby powder. Get some.”

"Of course!" Ozzi said, raising his finger. "So scatterbrained."

"Yeah, you sound like it." Bria smirked. Melonie slowly trailed behind the pair. She was fidgeting with her fingers and trying hard to fight the urge to pester Ozzi and Bria.

"In any case, have you spoken to that girl from the place that sells those scones you like so much?" Ozzi asked. "Maybe she could give you a massage," he said, chuckling.

"Yeah, me and Jazz aren't gonna work out," Bria replied. "She does make some bomb ass scones, though. I'll keep her around."

The trio exited the hangar, entering one of the many hallways of The Bureau. Blur Havok members ran past the leaders to manage their day-to-day activities and Bria and Ozzi casually greeted some of their allies as they passed them by. Melonie opened her mouth, but quickly snapped it shut. She rubbed the back of her neck.

"What about you?" Bria asked. "Gettin' any booty calls now that your arm's fixed?"

"I have neither the time nor the energy to spare for romantic relationships," Ozzi said. "In mere months, I managed to develop holographic communication and release the open-source blueprints to private corporations." Bria stared at Ozzi blankly. Nothing he was saying registered, but she let him continue. "The restoration of my arm is possibly the worst thing to happen to Valhalla."

Bria held a stern face as she tried to process what Ozzi meant. "Your arm being fixed is bad?"

"Hm. Phrasing was *not* the best there," Ozzi said. "What I meant was–"

Melonie finally burst. "Guys, I've got to ask you something."

"Is this an 'Alastor' question?" Bria asked without turning around. The trio continued down the hallway.

Ozzi looked at Bria with a shocked expression. "That's *my* line."

"Yes," Melonie said slowly. "Kind of."

Bria sighed. "Go ahead."

"I've been trying to tell Alastor something and it's kind of hard to say."

"Oh, my God, Melonie's pregnant." Bria gasped and turned to face Ozzi. The trio stopped and faced each other.

"No, no." Melonie shook her head. "It's not really a bad thing."

"You want a break?" Ozzi asked.

"That *is* a bad thing," Bria pointed out.

"No," Melonie said. "I'm thinking about the opposite, actually."

Bria's eyes widened so much that they practically popped out of her head. "You shittin' me?" she excitedly exclaimed.

"That's why I wanted to ask you guys about it," Melonie said. "Should I be feeling this way only two months in?"

Bria and Ozzi stopped walking and looked at each other. Bria placed her hand on her chin as she pondered. "I mean..."

"Biologically speaking, it is quite normal for romantic feelings to grow intensely over a short period of time," Ozzi said.

"But marriage, though?" Bria asked in a high-pitched, awkward voice.

"It's never been easy for me to fall in love. The... 'accident' made me feel so unattractive. I'm..." Melonie hesitated. "I'm basically half-robot with how many synthetic implants I need to keep me alive," she said. "But ever since Alastor and I were in college, I realized that I haven't felt this way about *anyone.*" Melonie began to glow lovingly thinking about him. "And he treats me so well in spite of that."

"Melonie, I'm pretty concerned here." Ozzi gulped. "That was a rough time for you. You could simply be experiencing side effects from your..." he paused and his eyes wandered nervously, "...depression."

"Let me ask you this," Bria pointed at Melonie. "Have you said you love him yet?"

Melonie did not respond. She folded her arms across her chest, trying to make herself smaller.

"Oh, my fuckin' God." Bria slapped her forehead and covered her face.

"Well, that's fine," Ozzi chimed in, reassuring Melonie. "If you really feel this way about him, start there."

"What if he doesn't feel the same way?" Melonie asked.

Bria and Ozzi looked at each other, then snickered. "We're pretty sure he does," Bria said, winking.

"Work up that courage and let him know how you feel." Ozzi smiled. Melonie warmly smiled back at her friends.

The Knights all filed into one room. Iskander was standing behind a large, black table that had an assortment of papers and folders strewn across it. He waited for everyone to step up to the table before speaking. "I've informed our father that The Legion will be striking soon."

"Yeah," Alastor said. "My team just confirmed that."

"But not in the way that we suspect," Iskander continued.

"Ryze has amassed a sizable force since the Vault Incident due to your actions," Roark said. "He used the idea that your actions were genocidal in nature to persuade Synthetics to join his cause."

"He is developing an ungodly new class of Ski'tal – we've been calling them Sleepers," Iskander said. "They have the ability to instantly disguise themselves as humans."

"Ryze will use them to slowly infiltrate NVC and destroy it from within," Roark said. "No one will be able to prepare for such an attack."

"Luckily for us, there are only a few Sleepers he's successfully deployed. We have time, but not much," Iskander said. Alastor looked at the floor, discouraged.

"It was the right thing to do," Roark said to Alastor. "Those monsters would have killed us all."

"Their forces now are preferable to what The Children of Ryze would have been," Iskander added. "If Ryze would have won in The Vault, there's no telling what we'd be subjected to at this point."

Alastor let out a long sigh. "Alright, what's the plan then?"

"Velanna's *questionable* methods of accessing your location and reports through the NVC Codex proved fruitful," Iskander said.

"That explains why you stole Ozzi's armor..." Alastor hissed. He glanced at Velanna and sneered but she simply wiggled her fingers back at him.

"We believe The Nexus is the key," Roark said.

"How?" Alastor asked. "I mean, sure, it's a database of Ski'tal life signs and coordinates across Valhalla, but all that's good for is finding Special Interest targets and being creepily invasive. Orwellian, but nothing we could use." He looked to Roark. "Is that really worth our time?"

"Yes." Sreda stepped up to the table. "The Nexus is a network just like any other. A live index of Ski'tal vitals could be forced to accept a connection in the opposite direction and affect the Ski'tal."

"That was surprisingly well-spoken," Alastor said. Sreda smiled giddily at him and he smiled back. He narrowed his eyes in thought. He had a feeling he might have just solved the puzzle surrounding Sreda, but that theory would have to wait.

"My synthetic implants could then communicate with The Nexus, killing the Legion," Roark said. Iskander averted his eyes.

"Well, then you would know that we don't have any indication as to where the Nexus is," Alastor said. "But I assume there's a plan for that."

"Not exactly," Malachi said.

"What?" Alastor said incredulously. Malachi only shrugged.

"That's why we needed you, Alastor," Iskander said. "We have dossiers and records of the event, but you and your team had firsthand experience with Ryze. You know how he operates and how he thinks."

"We've wasted enough time," Roark said. "Gather your team and devise a plan. Take your fellow Knights with you."

"What about you, dad?" Alastor asked.

"I will stay here. If I die, the plan fails." Roark leaned against the large table. "Come back when you can access The Nexus, and I will join you."

"That's all fine and dandy," Alastor said, glaring at Velanna, "but does *she* have to go with us?"

"*She* is an insurance policy. Her talents are formidable."

Alastor growled to himself. "Whatever. Let's head out," he said.

"I'll drive," Arashi said.

Roark looked at Arashi. "Thank you, son."

Arashi squashed his face in disgust. "Piss off." The hair on the back of Alastor's neck stood up, but he remained silent as Arashi led The Knights out of the room.

"This is going to be fun," Velanna said behind Alastor.

"I'm serious, I will cut your hand off."

Melonie, Bria, and Ozzi waited in the briefing room of The Bureau. Bria flipped her combat knife in the air several times while Melonie paced around the table. She had paced for so long that she was surely making a rut in the floor. Ozzi was catching up on one of the many tech magazines he had received in the mail that he never had a chance to read. The sound of several footsteps approached the briefing room and Melonie looked towards the entrance to see Alastor enter the room. She ran up to him and wrapped her arms tightly around him. Alastor stumbled backward as he caught her. "Hey, babe," Alastor said softly. He lifted Melonie's chin up to kiss her lips.

"Glad you made it back safe," Melonie said. She glanced up at The Knights standing behind Alastor – and Velanna, standing directly in front of them. Velanna grinned smugly at Melonie.

"Alastor," Melonie said with a wavering voice. "She's still here..."

"I am painfully aware." Alastor let go of Melonie. "Team, these are the Knights of Hacon. They will be working with us on this mission."

"Hol' up. 'The Knights of *what*?" Bria sheathed her knife and leapt to her feet.

"It's news to me too, don't worry."

Ozzi threw the magazine over his head. "Mission? You have information?"

"Yes." Alastor walked further into the room to make space for Velanna and the Knights. "Iskander, can you fill them in?"

"Certainly," Iskander said.

"This is quite the task," Ozzi said while stroking his beard. "Definitely not as straightforward as The Vault. Target unknown."

"Where do you think Ryze would store information *that* important?" Malachi asked.

"Chained to his wrist," Melonie responded.

"Yes, but that would be stupid," Sreda added. "If something were to unexist him, then The Nexus would be permanently inaccessible."

Alastor forced himself to ignore Sreda's eccentric way of speaking, choosing instead to just nod in agreement with her. "Ryze is practical. He'd only give that information to his most trusted personnel."

"Aha!" Ozzi blurted out. "Ryze is practical, yes, but also *emotional.* He would have constant tabs on where that information is accessible."

"So, what we need to do is find the receipts," Bria surmised. "Sounds great but, knowin' Ryze, he'd be on us like white on rice the moment we touch one of 'em."

"Sounds simple," Iskander said. "We'll make two teams–"

"I'm mad you're just making the plan like this ain't *my* house," Alastor joked.

Iskander sighed and continued. "Team A will infiltrate the base and get the intel. Team B will be on standby to create a distraction and receive Team A when they complete the mission."

"Awesome. Can't wait to go toe-to-toe with Ryze." Arashi cracked his knuckles.

"Says the guy who hasn't fought Ryze before," Alastor said. "It's easier said than done."

Velanna raised her hand from the corner of the room, only just now deciding to contribute to the plan. "I know where we can start."

Alastor sighed. “Where, Velanna?”

“His home.”

Chapter 4

"Alastor, can we talk?" Melonie asked.

The couple had stepped away from the rest of the group to allow a little more privacy. The couple walked down the hallway. "What's up? Something in my teeth?" Alastor asked, pointing to his mouth.

"Alastor, it's serious," Melonie frowned.

"Sorry, I always make jokes when I'm nervous," Alastor said as he quickly sobered up.

"We haven't really had a chance to have a heart-to-heart in a while."

"True. What's on your mind?"

Melonie's heart started beating against her chest. "Remember when we talked in the Vault? About..." Melonie trailed off, obviously discomforted by the memory.

"Ah. Yeah." The couple stopped walking and faced each other.

"Well, I don't feel like that anymore." Melonie held Alastor's hands. "I haven't felt like that since then."

"I mean, I don't wanna take all the credit for that, but..." Alastor smirked.

"You deserve all the credit, Alastor."

Alastor's eyes widened. "Wow, Melonie. I— uh..."

"I understand if it's a bit much. But it's true," Melonie looked up to Alastor with a twinkle in her eye.

Alastor stared into Melonie's eyes and smiled softly. "Is that the look you said I had that day?"

"Could be." Melonie released Alastor's hands. He stared silently at her.

"I—"

"Excuse me!" Velanna called out.

Melonie and Alastor jumped as Velanna's shrill voice snapped them out of their trance. Alastor turned to address Velanna. "What?" he asked harshly.

"Ozzi would like a word with you." Velanna raised a finger. "Also, restroom?"

Melonie threw her thumb over her shoulder. "It's at the end of the hallway."

Alastor groaned. "We'll put a pin in this, Mel. Sorry, babe." He strode past Velanna and into the briefing room. Velanna began to make her way towards the restroom, but she stopped and eyed Melonie. She stood over her like a mother about to scold her child. Melonie waited for Velanna to speak, but she didn't.

"Uh..." Melonie awkwardly started. The Blur Havok members continued to hustle and bustle through the hallways. "Did you need something?"

Velanna snickered through her nose. "You're Melonie, right?"

"Yeah..."

"What a pretty little thing you are."

Melonie nervously chuckled. "Thanks?"

Velanna's face soured. "I've heard so *little* about you. Let's keep it that way." She smirked and strode past her. Melonie stared at Velanna in disbelief as she watched her walk down the hallway. *At least she's actually going to the restroom,* she thought as she turned and made her way to the briefing room. She walked past Alastor and Ozzi discussing strategies as she made her way around the room.

"We'll need heavy weaponry on Ryze to keep him in place," Ozzi said.

"Sounds like that'll be a job for you and Arashi," Alastor replied.

Arashi walked up to Ozzi. "I blow shit up."

"Ah! A fellow demolitions expert?" Ozzi sounded pleased.

"No, I'm a *munitions* expert."

Ozzi looked at Alastor, concerned. Alastor just smiled. "That's your man."

"So, you like weapons?" Ozzi asked for clarification.

"Yes." Arashi folded his arms impatiently.

Ozzi covered his mouth. "Note to self: keep Arashi out of Tech Lab," he muttered.

"I can hear you."

Ozzi looked perplexed. "Doesn't matter. It's called a 'note to self' not a 'note to possible project wrecking arsonist'!"

"You guys will get along just fine," Alastor said cheerfully. He patted Ozzi on the back and walked away, only to be greeted by Bria.

"Bro," Bria said.

"B," Alastor jokingly responded.

"Me and Iskander were talkin' and decided who should be on Team A and Team B."

"Uh-huh..."

"Look, I'm sorry. I tried," Bria said. "Team B is Ozzi, Arashi, Iskander, Sreda, and me..." Alastor stared at Bria blankly. "Team A is you, Melonie, Malachi, and... *Velanna.*"

Alastor covered his face. "This has got to be an out-of-season April Fool's joke."

"Weirdly specific. Anyways," Bria wrapped her arm around Alastor's shoulders and brought him close, "If shit goes south and you and bitchtits get into it, you and Melonie could beat the bricks off her easily."

Alastor looked around with anxiety in his eyes. "She's got tricks up her sleeve, Bria. It wouldn't be that easy."

The color drained from Bria's face as she heard the uncertainty in Alastor's voice. "Maybe if I help...?" she muttered sheepishly.

"Your best bet is to *be me,*" Alastor whispered, ignoring Bria. "If you're not me, don't *ever* turn your back on that woman." He stalked off without another word. Bria looked at the door to see Velanna walk in and examine the room with her signature smile. She hid behind Iskander before Velanna could see her.

Alastor spotted Sreda examining Ozzi's blueprints. "Something on your mind, sis?" Alastor asked.

"Your technology is quite primitive," she said.

"Excuse me?" Ozzi overheard.

"Don't get him started," Alastor sighed with a knowing chuckle.

Sreda turned to Ozzi. "Primitive. Defined as the character of an early stage in the evolutionary—?"

"Yeah, yeah, yeah, I know what it means. Don't patronize me," Ozzi said, his face turning a light shade of red. "What exactly makes my tech 'primitive'?"

"Your armor lacks optimization," Sreda stated with the eloquence of a professor. Ozzi scoffed. "You could move the couplers to a much more fortifiable position," she continued, pointing to a spot on the blueprint. "You sever this coupler with, say, a slice from Ryze's wrist-mounted blade, and power will be cut to the left half of the suit."

Ozzi stared at her with his jaw hanging open. "I don't care if you're right, you shut the hell up."

"Not my fault you made a dumb." Sreda covered her mouth.

"Rich, coming from the jerk who thinks 'dumb' is a noun." Ozzi walked away. "Don't say shit about my tech again."

"I didn't mean to say 'dumb'…" Sreda scratched her head, embarrassed.

Alastor examined Sreda again, putting more pieces together. He patted her on the back to comfort her. "Don't worry about it. He'll be fine."

"Melonie told me that the Council has approved our liaison." Iskander walked up to Alastor. "Are you ready to begin the mission?"

"M'kay, yeah, so I have a question," Alastor started.

"Is it about the criminal, Velanna, being on your team?"

"Hell yes, it is! Can we not?"

"Look, if it were up to me, she'd be locked in a freight container on its way to the U.S." Iskander leaned in. "But dad promised her one thing: a chance to get to *you.* It's part of her contract."

"Why in the—?" Alastor hesitated as he spotted Velanna standing behind Melonie, Malachi, Arashi, and Bria. She raised her hand to her ear.

"You're looking handsome as ever, Jack. Come here and talk to me," Velanna said in a private channel over the comms. "I promise I won't bite."

"Who the fu—?" Alastor sighed. "Who gave Velanna access to our comms relay?" he calmly asked.

"Not sure," Iskander said. "She must've figured it out herself. If it's any consolation, I'm keeping my eye on her too."

"That's all anyone can do with her..." Alastor groaned.

Alastor walked with Melonie, Malachi, and Velanna to the transports. "Team A is heading out," Melonie said over the comms. "Once we have the intel we need we can proceed to phase two."

Velanna lead the group to the transports and Alastor stared at the back of her head, waiting for her to make an unauthorized move. "I'll drive," Alastor said.

"Shotgun!" Velanna said.

"Malachi's driving," Alastor spat back. He chucked the vehicle's key fob over his head and Malachi barely caught it.

"Okay then, anyone got directions?" Malachi said.

"The last known location of the Legion Headquarters was in The Wolves' Den," Melonie said as she examined a holographic map above her wrist. "A borough in The Slums."

Alastor felt a jolt in his spine. "Haven't heard that name in years."

"You know about it?" Malachi asked as they reached a small SUV.

"Yeah." Alastor opened one of the rear doors for Melonie. "An S3 mission went bad there."

Velanna sat in the front passenger seat. "Based on what I read, the mission was a success," she said.

"For the Synthetic Oppression Squad, sure." Alastor sat in the SUV next to Melonie.

"Don't you mean the Synthetic Suppression Squad?" Malachi naively asked. He pressed the ignition button and the vehicle revved to life.

"I meant what I said," Alastor coldly retorted.

Ryze stood in an unlit chamber. His vibrant, emerald eyes glowed in the dark room as he examined a tablet, his face lit up by the harsh, white luminescence of the screen. He tapped the display a few times, reading it silently. Ryze grunted to himself and raised his hand to the side of his head. "Officer Luht, come in," he said calmly over the comms.

"Yes, sir?" a drone nervously replied. He sounded unprepared and unsettled by Ryze's sudden call.

Ryze placed the tablet on a nearby table. "I need eyes on Councilor Vasquez."

Velanna and Alastor held hands as the couple walked through a park on a beautiful spring day. The colorful flora that surrounded them flourished under the heat of the sun. The path rounded a pond, where a paddling of ducks was swimming in the water. Velanna gasped and pointed at the ducks.

"Aw, look at them!" Velanna cooed. "Aren't they adorable?"

"Yeah, they are," Alastor agreed. His phone vibrated in his pocket, but he ignored it.

"Jack, when you leave Blur Havok," Velanna babbled in a cutesy voice, "do you think you'd want kids?"

Alastor smiled. "Sure. Maybe later. I don't wanna rush, though."

"They'd be fine without you?"

"I think so. Jason's been doing a great job of leading Blur Havok since I got to Valhalla."

"And Bria?"

"My apprentice is doing good enough without me." Alastor and Velanna stopped at a bench and sat. "I taught her well."

"That's good," Velanna said, nodding her head. "I just want a normal life. White picket fence, kids, dog, and an amazing husband." She smiled and rubbed Alastor's hand.

Alastor tilted his head. "And you think that's me?"

"Well, yeah," Velanna said. "No one wants you like I do."

"I'm flattered, but there's a few things you have to do on your end." Alastor's phone vibrated again, but the conversation he was having was more important to him than whatever was on his phone.

"I know," Velanna said. "It's just that—"

"C'mon, Velanna," Alastor said impatiently. "No excuses."

"Okay, Jack..." Velanna watched the ducks swim around the pond and Alastor pulled out his phone. He activated the screen and his heart stopped. There were two missed calls from Melonie Sanders. She had shown no romantic interest in him during their last conversation, but his heart still secretly longed for her. And yet, he was with Velanna – a woman who actually wanted him. Alastor felt a massive lump in his throat.

He reluctantly slid his phone back into his pocket and looked up at Velanna. She gleefully smiled at him and Alastor weakly smiled back. A wave of emotions flooded his head as he remembered his feelings for Melonie.

"Alastor?" Melonie said, gently shaking his shoulder.

Alastor had a blank expression on his face as a single tear rolled down his cheek. He snapped back to the present day and looked at Melonie. "Huh?"

"Are you okay?" Melonie asked.

"Yeah, just—" Alastor wiped the tear away. "I just, uh... was thinking about something." He looked at Velanna.

She smirked at him like she knew what he had been thinking about, before turning her head back to the front of the vehicle.

"Do you want to talk about it?" Melonie asked.

"No, it's cool. It's in the past." Alastor's voice darkened as he glared at Velanna. "Where it belongs."

"We're in the mission area." Malachi put the SUV in park. "Who's on point?"

"Velanna," Alastor said. "Since this is her crazy-ass idea."

"Of course," she said. "Wouldn't want it any other way." Velanna stepped out of the SUV and closed the door. Malachi, Melonie, and Alastor followed her lead.

Malachi walked up to Alastor and the two brothers walked side-by-side. "You guys sure do have some history," he said. "Would you ever forgive her?"

"Fuck no," Alastor responded bluntly.

"Okay then," Malachi said awkwardly. "What about dad? I know how you feel about him."

Alastor felt a lump in his throat. "I want to," he started, "but it's hard, you know?"

"No, not really." Alastor glared at Malachi with narrowed eyes. "I've always known and cared about him," Malachi continued. "It's hard for me to say otherwise."

Melonie joined Alastor on the other side. "I mean, if you don't care about him, what was up with the waterworks back when we first met?"

Alastor averted his eyes and looked at the ground. "I– uh..." Alastor rubbed his temple and sighed. "Look, man. No one *wants* to hate their dad. I do care about him."

"So the yelling and the screaming...?" Malachi raised an eyebrow.

"I was... emotional," Alastor sheepishly said. "It's been years' man. Last memory I have of my dad was him packing his shit and leaving me and my mom to struggle. You could understand why I'd be pissed."

Malachi stared at Alastor. "Huh. That sucks man. I'm sure there's more to it, though."

"Of course." Alastor glanced at Melonie. She looked up at him and innocently smiled. Alastor smiled back. "So," he turned his attention back to Malachi. "What about you? How do you see dad?"

"I'd do anything for him," Malachi continued.

"That's not healthy," Alastor said as he pulled his SCAR rifle from his back.

"Well, I can't think of anything to knock him for. He's never done me wrong."

"Huh." Alastor scanned the young sniper. "I guess I understand your perspective."

"Our dad is a great man," Malachi said. "I want him to look at me the way he looks at Iskander or Sreda."

"Hm." Alastor processed what Malachi said. "You might need to get out more."

Malachi scoffed. "You're just mad I have goals to accomplish."

"I didn't know dickriding was a goal." Melonie chortled loudly before quickly covering her mouth.

Malachi groaned. "I get enough of this shit from Arashi..."

"Look, look, look," Alastor interrupted. "All I'm saying is that there's more to life than just brown-nosing our dad, y'know?"

"You might want to tell that to dad."

Alastor faltered. "What?"

"You should have heard how much he talked about you. 'Alastor this, Alastor that, Alastor will make the family complete'. I was starting to think I'd have to compete with you too," he said. Malachi paused for a moment before continuing. "But in any case, he loves you, that's for sure," he said with a bit more tact.

Alastor was stunned. There was more to his father than he thought. He smiled. "That's... that's good to know, bro."

The trio caught up to Velanna, who was standing at a steep hill. A large fortress made of makeshift steel plates and metal sheets awaited them below; it looked like the giant base was composed of several smaller outposts. “Anybody want to knock?” Velanna quipped.

“Alright guys,” Alastor said. “Keep it quiet. Take ‘em out only if we have to.”

“I'll provide overwatch on this hill.” Malachi armed himself with his Model 700 sniper rifle. “I'll hit you up if anything goes down.”

“You got it, kid,” Alastor said. “Move out, team.”

Alastor, Melonie, and Velanna slid down the hill and into cover behind a wall of rusted sheet metal. Velanna poked her head around the cover and held up three fingers.

Alastor peeked over the edge of the trio’s cover. The three guards conversed with each other while standing in front of the entrance to the base. They were not going to be moving anytime soon.

“Malachi, take out these guards,” Alastor whispered.

“On it,” Malachi said over the comms. Five suppressed sniper shots came from the top of the hill. The sound of Ski'tal bodies hitting the ground indicated that they were clear to move up.

“Kid's a good shot – but Bria would've done it in two.” Alastor smiled as they moved to new cover.

"This is like The Vault all over again," Melonie stated.

"You two know how to have fun, then." Velanna smirked. "Wish I got in on whatever was going on there."

"Take care of those bodies," Alastor ordered Velanna, just to get her to be quiet. "The moment they see a dead body, we're screwed."

"Why not you?" Velanna sassed. "You're the one who can teleport."

"Again – *your* crazy-ass plan."

"Fair enough," Velanna said.

"Heads up, Team A," Iskander said over the comms. "Blur Havok scouts are reporting that Ryze is in Downtown Slums. You have approximately 45 minutes."

"Roger that," Alastor said. "Ryze's quarters should be in the most heavily guarded area of the base."

"Then we have to move quickly and quietly," Melonie said.

Velanna finished dragging the bodies out of the way and positioned them under a pile of rubbish. "We gotta move," Alastor said to Velanna. "Take out any contacts on our way and try to hide the bodies." Alastor pulled out his sword.

"Don't have to hide a body if there isn't one." Velanna smiled.

Alastor groaned. "Whatever. Melonie, you're on point."

The trio entered the front gate and silently moved through the base, slipping in and out of alleys and around piles of crates. Ski'tal drones patrolled the base with their rifles at low ready. There was a large building with a black and red triangular roof painted in spotty, but solid-colored streaks – the house colors of the Ski'tal Legion. A Ski'tal stood in front of the double doors that lead inside.

Alastor smiled. "Let me try something. Duck."

Velanna and Melonie dropped down to the ground as Alastor deployed his shield and flung it at the guard, striking him in the face. He dropped to the ground, unconscious, and the shield fell to the dirt ground. "Not really the best time to try new things, but good work," Melonie said.

They ran up to the unconscious guard and Melonie and Alastor stacked up on the side of the building's double doors. Alastor peeked into the room beyond the door and counted four Ski'tal. Suddenly, a series of sickening slicing sounds came from behind them, startling Alastor. He looked back to see the Ski'tal guard mangled and barely recognizable. Velanna dropped the head of the drone and smiled coyly at them.

"Add *that* to the list of unnecessary things done today..." Melonie muttered.

"Velanna, we're about to breach and clear. I count four drones. No guns," Alastor said. "We clear this room and we can catch our bearings."

"Excellent. On your mark, Jack," Velanna said.

Alastor nodded, ignoring Velanna's use of his former alias. He burst into the room, shield first, and rammed into the closest Ski'tal, sending the drone flying into the wall. Melonie threw a dagger into the head of another drone on Alastor's left while Velanna grabbed a drone behind him and snapped her neck. The fourth drone raised his rifle to Velanna's head, but Alastor's broadsword impaled him in the face, pinning him to the wall behind Velanna.

"You really are a knight in shining armor," Velanna joked.

"Shut up." Alastor stomped over to his sword and pulled it out of the wall. Alastor quietly forced the double doors closed. "He was going to do me a solid, but that would have jeopardized the mission." Alastor collapsed his shield and placed it back onto his forearm. "Any intel, Melonie?"

"Looks like we're in some kind of briefing area." Melonie shuffled around some papers and tablets on a huge, circular wooden table. There were six metal chairs surrounding the table. "I've got something," she said. She pulled a piece of paper close to her face and adjusted her glasses. "Says here some non-aligned humans attacked Ryze's personal quarters with Molotov cocktails. The damage hasn't been repaired yet."

"Oh, no, they're aligned," Velanna said. "Just not with you. 'Dirt Hounds' they call themselves. They hate anything related to the Ski'tal."

"Why do you know about them?" Alastor asked.

"They pay very, *very* handsomely." Velanna grinned. "I know a few of them."

"I'd expect no less from the likes of you," Alastor scoffed.

Iskander, Bria, and Sreda stood at the briefing room table. Iskander was reading one of Ozzi's magazines – something about weapon reloading techniques and ammunition cartridges. Bria was playing a game on her phone but the banal nature of the game bored her. She looked at Sreda's legs and saw an opportunity to strike up a conversation. "So, I gotta ask. What's up with those legs?"

"A personal choice," Sreda muttered.

Bria looked at Sreda dumbfounded. "Why would you wanna chop your legs off like that?"

"I have phases, so to imply," Sreda said. She seemed to be having trouble socializing with Bria.

"What, like a girl who thinks she's bisexual just 'cause she doesn't understand men?" Bria laughed, oblivious to Sreda's discomfort.

"No." Sreda did not explain further and, instead, shrank into herself.

Bria looked at Sreda, utterly confused. "Uh-huh..."

Arashi entered the room. "Bria, Ozzi wanted me to give you this." He placed an M110 sniper rifle on the table.

"Ooh shit! New toy!" Bria grabbed the rifle and proceeded to press and pull on the different components of the gun.

Arashi looked at her warmly. "You look kinda cute when you're happy."

Bria stopped in place and stared at Arashi. She slowly began to giggle. "No one told him, did they?" Bria asked Sreda and Iskander. Iskander looked down at the table where a tablet with a red blinking light sat and he hastily grabbed it.

"Tell me what?" Arashi asked with a slight smile.

Bria laughed. "Nigga, you barkin' up the wrong tree."

Iskander read the tablet. "Shit," he muttered. "We've gotta go," he said to the rest of the team.

Melonie peeked out of the door. "We're clear."

"Melonie, cloak and search for Ryze's quarters," Alastor ordered. "We'll back you up once you confirm. Any important information, I'll switch to your personal channel."

Melonie nodded, then looked at the smiling Velanna. Her Cheshire cat grin gave Melonie goosebumps. *Yeah, she's creepy.* She pulled out a hood from the back of her armor and hid under it, quickly fading into transparency. From Alastor and Velanna's viewpoint, the door opened and closed on its own as Melonie left the room.

"Now that we're alone," Velanna said, "I've been meaning to tell you how much I've missed you."

"I'd like to think that if I shot you, I wouldn't miss you," Alastor confidently said with a condescending smile.

Velanna ignored Alastor. "So, this Melonie girl. She let you be alone with me?"

"Yes, because it's not hard for her to beat out a conniving loser like you."

Velanna sucked her teeth. "Jack, that's hurtful."

"That's the point."

The Ski'tal were none the wiser to her presence as Melonie walked through the base. Each step she took was muffled, barely discernable to the drones in the room. Melonie scanned each surface, looking for signs of damage that would distinguish Ryze's quarters from the rest.

If dating Alastor has taught me anything, it's that he sent me out here because it's probably safer than being with that girl. I wonder what her damage is... Melonie found a surface with a large, gnarled scorch mark on it. *Bingo.*

"Babe, go ahead and find that intel," Alastor said over the comms. "I'm getting word on a developing situation."

"Got it," Melonie whispered.

One of the drones nearby whipped around and faced Melonie. He pointed at the Ski'tal behind her and barked in Skigon. Melonie halted. The responding drone shook his head and the two continued their respective patrols. Melonie sighed and continued to move.

She circled around the building until she found a metal door that led inside. Melonie checked to make sure no one was watching before she tried to open the large wooden door, but it didn't budge and she accidentally rammed into it instead. Her little body made a large thud when her shoulder slammed into the door. *Shit.* Melonie glanced around to see if anyone heard her slip-up. After a few seconds of waiting for a response, she unsheathed a dagger, forcefully stabbed the lock on the door, and twisted it with concentrated effort. The lock ripped open, destroying the mechanism inside. Melonie tried the handle again and the door opened easily. She de-cloaked as soon as it closed behind her.

Melonie scanned the firelit room. The fur of some unearthly beast lay on the floor. The six-legged animal had beady, black eyes, dark turquoise fur, and large, ram-like horns with tusks protruding from its underbite. Melonie had no clue what this beast was or how Ryze had even obtained its fearsome pelt. Large tapestries hung from the walls, each with large, Skigon characters on them. Ski'tal heirlooms and paintings decorated the remaining walls and shelves, and the head of a petrified Ski'tal was mounted on one of the walls. Melonie walked closer to the bust. "*Ist Nel Bav Kast*" was written in Skigon underneath. "Glory until the end," Melonie translated.

She continued to examine the room and came across a desk with a tablet. She picked it up and poked the screen a few times before ejecting a plug from the wrist of her armor and plugging it into the bottom of the tablet. Melonie found a file labeled "Nexus" and she quickly scrolled through it and found that it contained twelve Skigon names, followed by coordinates. As she transferred the intel from the tablet, Melonie looked up and spotted a small doll sitting on a shelf. It had gray burlap skin, a fluffy blue tuft of hair, and purple felt clothes. Its simple, tiny smile greeted Melonie innocently. She paused. *That... looks like...*

"Melonie," Alastor said over the comms, the sound of gunfire ringing in the background. "We've gotta move!"

Melonie heard a massive thump right outside the door. She ejected the plug from the tablet and threw it back onto the desk before re-cloaking.

Suddenly, the door swung open and Ryze stepped in with a scowl.

Chapter 5

Alastor and Velanna waited patiently in the briefing area, not talking.

"Jack," Velanna said, breaking the silence. "You think about us, don't you?" Alastor's heart twisted and he stepped further away from Velanna.

"I know you do. The look on your face when we were on the way here? Speaks louder than anything you could ever say."

"Velanna," Alastor's voice broke. "You just don't fucking get it, do you?" He turned to look at her with tears in his eyes and Velanna looked back, stunned.

"When I think about what we had, I'm not happy," Alastor said, his voice still wavering.
Velanna placed her hand on her chest and regretfully looked away. "I feel pain when I think about you, Velanna."

Velanna stuttered. "Why?"

"What you promised me was a *lie.*"

Velanna's shoulders sunk and she averted her eyes. "I didn't lie."

"I wanted a normal life and you did everything you could to make sure that couldn't happen," Alastor continued, ignoring her. "And now that I'm finally happy, you wanna pull this shit and drudge up these old ass feelings."

Velanna sniffed as tears began to roll down her face. "You know I care about you, Alastor."

"You do? Then once we're done with this mission, *fuck off.*" Static scratched in Alastor's ear and he moved around the room to get better reception.

"—eam A, come in!" Bria yelled over the comms.

"What is it?" Alastor asked, worry filling his voice.

"We've got several contacts en route to your position! Ski'tal *and* human!"

"Shit," Alastor muttered. "Dirt Hounds." He looked at Velanna, who was sulking near the door. "Roger, Bria. Melonie's getting the intel. Rendezvous with Malachi. We'll provide cover for Melonie." Alastor switched to Melonie's personal frequency. "Babe, go ahead and find that intel," Alastor said over the comms. "I'm getting word of a developing situation."

"Got it," Melonie whispered back.

"Alastor, check up!" Malachi said over comms. "I'm seeing activity moving towards the base. They are *not Ski'tal!*"

"Understood. Thanks, Malachi. Proceed to engage as soon as Team B arrives." Alastor drew his SCAR rifle from his back. He glared at Velanna. "We're making a distraction. You done with the crocodile tears?"

Velanna wiped her face and straightened before drawing her shotgun. "On you."

Alastor burst through the doors and fired his rifle into the air, alerting every Ski'tal in the area. They all turned to Alastor and Velanna.

"Hacon!" they yelled in unison. The drones rushed Velanna and Alastor.

"Don't know why," Alastor said, smiling. "But it feels kinda good to hear that again."

Alastor warped into the charging legion. He reappeared in the midst of the crowd and kneed a drone in the chin, sending him flying. Alastor deployed his shield and blocked a buckshot blast from a drone's shotgun. He shoved the barrel of his rifle into the drone's mouth and fired a burst of full-auto lead into his face, turning it into Swiss cheese. A drone suddenly kicked Alastor in the back, knocking him down. He rolled over onto his back to find the barrel of a rifle in his face. Before Alastor could defend himself, the drone's gut exploded, sending blue blood and organs through the air. The bisected drone dropped dead and Velanna rushed to Alastor, offering her hand. Velanna had a restrained smile on her face as swaths of Ski'tal appeared to be spontaneously dying behind her, dust and blood obscuring the cause of their deaths. Alastor stared at her hand and raised his own, palm facing Velanna. "I'm good," he said, rejecting her help as he picked himself up. Velanna nodded, silently accepting Alastor's rejection.

The two stood back to back, cutting down waves of Ski'tal. Velanna pulled out her G43X pistol and double-tapped four drones. Alastor let loose a spray of bullets and managed to fell six drones before his rifle's chamber locked open. He placed his rifle on his back as he hunkered down behind his shield. Velanna turned around and shot a group of slugs from her shotgun over Alastor's shield, blasting the rushing drones to bits. Alastor stood up and swatted two drones away with his shield.

"Thanks," Alastor said.

"No problem." Velanna smiled. "Y'know, we make a pretty good team."

"A'ight, chill out."

Alastor heard the sound of trucks revving in the distance and he looked to the entrance just as two beat-down pickup trucks with machine gun turrets on their beds burst through the gate. Humans in desert camouflage, tactical gear, and plate carriers manned the turrets, aiming at Blur Havok operatives and Ski'tal drones. "Shit! Technicals!" Alastor yelled. Velanna and Alastor scattered to their own cover behind metal plates as the machine guns sprayed a ludicrous amount of bullets at the drones, Velanna, and Alastor. The drones practically disintegrated as high-caliber bullets thumped against Alastor's cover.

"Melonie," Alastor said over the comms, the sound of gunfire nearly obscuring his voice. "We've gotta move!"

Melonie stood perfectly still as Ryze scanned the room with a sneer. He shrugged before quickly stomping to a nearby closet and yanking it open. Melonie held her breath. The sound of gunfire could be heard in the distance, but it wasn't loud enough to cover any noise she could possibly make.

Ryze grabbed rockets and boxes of bullets, mumbling something under his breath as he continued stocking up on ammunition. He opened a compartment hidden inside both of his arms and stashed the packets away. He punched the air with both fists and the panels on his arms snapped shut.

Melonie couldn't hold her breath any longer. She exhaled as slowly as she could, then inhaled at the same rate. Ryze quickly turned his head in Melonie's direction and began carefully walking towards her. Melonie tensed up immediately, trembling with each step Ryze took – but he walked right past her and stopped at the shelf to her right. He delicately picked up the doll and brought it close to his face, nuzzling his forehead against the doll's. Melonie was so close to Ryze that she could feel the intense heat from the vents and hear the exhausts of his folded wings softly purring.

Ryze hummed to himself before placing the doll back on the shelf. Without a second thought, he marched to the door as his right arm began transforming into a rocket launcher. He examined the lock on his door, then looked back into his room, but nothing seemed to be out of order. "I'll fix it later," he muttered angrily. He slammed the door behind him. Melonie recoiled as the sound barrier broke right outside of the door, violently shaking the room.

Melonie exhaled sharply as she decloaked. "Jesus Christ..." Melonie sighed. "Alastor, Ryze is here," she said to Alastor through the comms.

"I know!" Alastor yelled. An explosion boomed in the background. Melonie could feel the shockwave from her location. "Just what we fuckin' needed! Get the intel and head to Malachi's location!"

"What about you?" Melonie stammered. "Wh—What about the plan?"

"This *is* the plan!" The sound of metal clashing together reverberated over Alastor's comm system. "Sonovabitch!"

Melonie sighed. "Okay, Alastor. Stay safe." She quickly exited the room.

Alastor reloaded his rifle and slapped the bolt release. He peeked out of cover, barrel first, and discharged two rounds out of his rifle. A human on the back of one of the technicals flew backwards in a mist of red liquid. Alastor looked over and saw the other technical's turret turn to him and begin spinning. He ducked down as the bullets sprayed over him, pelting his safe space with hot metal. Over the sound of chaos, the crack of the sound barrier exploded above them, reverberating across the sky like a thunderclap.

"Hey!" Alastor yelled at Velanna. "Take cover!"

"Alastor, Ryze is here," Melonie said in Alastor's ear. The whistle of rockets raised the hair on Alastor's neck.

"I know!" Alastor yelled. Two gigantic thumps rocked Alastor's core as a fiery explosion engulfed both of the technicals, sending shrapnel flying over his head and grazing the shield on his back. The sound dampeners in his comm system barely saved his hearing from the deafening explosion. "Just what we fuckin' needed! Get the intel and head to Malachi's location!"

"What about you?" Melonie quietly stuttered. "Wh—What about the plan?"

"This *is* the plan!" A sharp blade ripped through Alastor's refuge, exposing him, and a large metal claw grabbed Alastor from the collar of his armor. "Sonovabitch!"

"How interesting," Ryze said. "The Dirt Hounds have competition."

Bria sat in the passenger seat of a military Humvee as Iskander drove ninety miles per hour through the streets of The Slums. Ozzi stood in the turret in the center of the Humvee and Arashi sat in the seat next to him, handing him 40-millimeter grenades to load into the turret. Sreda sat on the opposite side of Arashi, projecting a map from the palm of her synthetic hand. "Unknown human faction and flying bogey converging on Wolves' Den," Sreda said. "Death fight is imminent."

"This is not going according to plan," Iskander muttered as he swerved around a bend in the road and crashed through the corner of an abandoned house.

Bria smiled. "Nothing ever goes accordin' to plan around here." Her voice bounced as the Humvee rumbled down the road. She loaded a magazine into her sniper rifle and yanked the charging handle, chambering a round. "It just wouldn't be fun if it did."

"So, what's the plan when we get there?" Arashi asked. Iskander glanced at Bria and waited for a response.

Bria's heart dropped. This mission was hers to command. "Ah... shit," she whispered. The weight of responsibility sat heavily on her shoulders. Her breathing became labored as she realized that this wasn't just some recon mission – this was all-out warfare. Her mind began racing and she thought back to The Vault. The mission was hers back then too, and she hadn't known if Alastor would live through it. *"I'm proud of you. No matter what happens,"* Alastor's voice echoed in her head.

Her confidence came back in full force and a fearless grin spread across her face. "When we get to the mission area, we extract Melonie, give Alastor some covering fire, and put a hole in anything that isn't us." Bria turned to Arashi in the back seat. "Arashi, you and Ozzi will lay down some hate on Ryze as soon as you see those ugly green eyes."

Arashi smiled. "Sounds like my kinda plan."

"And if they change to red?" Ozzi peered down from the turret to speak.

"Shoot harder." Bria smirked.

Sreda was tinkering with the hologram projecting out of her palm. She looked through it and saw Bria's eyes on her. She froze, suddenly nervous to speak.

"Sreda, you find Melonie and get her back to the truck."

Sreda swallowed and mustered up a few words. "Save the little one. Affirmative," she replied.

"Iskander, you'll have to get down and dirty with Ryze and those human bastards. Even the close-quarters odds." Iskander silently nodded.

"I'll provide suppressive fire with Malachi. Keep the softer targets in one spot," Bria said.

Team A's SUV quickly came into view, with Malachi lying nearby, covering fire. Iskander slammed on the brakes and the tires screeched loudly as the vehicle came skidding to a halt, right at the edge of the cliff.

"Team B, bring the noise!" Bria bellowed.

Bria, Iskander, Sreda, and Arashi all hopped out of the Humvee, armed to the teeth. The gates to The Wolves' Den were torn open and two charred, flaming technicals sat in front of them. Bria spotted Ryze holding Alastor up by his armor. She growled and aimed down her scope, effortlessly aligning the crosshairs with Ryze's back, and fired two bullets.

Ryze lurched forward as a large gush of cyan blood squirted out of his back. The bullet flew straight through his breastplate and he grabbed his chest, dropping Alastor. Ryze looked up at Bria, then at the destroyed gate as more Dirt Hounds charged the compound, followed by three more technicals. Ryze sounded the alarm from a panel on his wrist and Legion forces poured from all directions of the massive base. Humans and Ski'tal alike dropped to the ground as bullets were fired from every which way.

Bria looked out across the madness. "This is one massive clusterfu—"

A rocket-powered grenade spiraled over Bria's head, trailing smoke as it rocketed into the sky above her, and she instinctively ducked down. "Holy shit," she muttered to herself.

Alastor scrambled away from Ryze and engaged his shield as Ryze charged at him, deploying his twin wrist blades.

"I see you got rid of Fel's old blade." Alastor rolled backward as Ryze stabbed the hard-packed dirt. "Good. It was clashing. I think you should stay within your color palette."

"It's in a safe place," Ryze played along. "My love's blade deserves better than such utilitarian usage."

"Sounds more like you're moving on." Alastor drew his sword and slashed Ryze's calf. "That's healthy, Ryze."

Ryze cried out in pain and knelt down to grab his calf as cyan blood leaked from the wound. "You caught me on a good—" Ryze paused as he heard someone approach from behind him. His battle mask closed over his face and he turned to face his new opponent as a shotgun blast hit him in the face. Velanna gulped as Ryze stood up, looming over her. "The criminal." Ryze swung his forearm into Velanna's gut and pinned her against a nearby wall, crushing her. "An alliance was made between you and this wretched scum? How *desperate*."

"Alastor!" Velanna rasped. "Help me!"

Alastor froze as a wicked thought entered his head. Velanna had been nothing but the bane of his existence and, for just this one moment, he thought about letting Ryze break every bone in her body. After all, it was not *his hands* that would have blood on them.

Who would miss her?

Before Alastor could make a decision, a large armored blur tackled Ryze, freeing Velanna. She hugged her ribs and looked up at Alastor with anger in her eyes. Alastor silently stared at Velanna, sword in hand.

Melonie ran unseen through the Ski'tal base as Legion troops ran past her. She looked up and saw Bria and the rest of Team B on the ridge firing down on the clash below.

Before Melonie could get her bearings, a Ski'tal ran straight into her. Melonie's cloak slipped off of her as they both fell to the ground in a tangle of synthetic and human limbs. As the Ski'tal regained his senses, he focused his eyes on Melonie and, suddenly realizing what she was, cried out in alarmed Skigon. "Shit," she muttered. Melonie leapt up and dashed into the midst of the battle, pulling out her P226 pistol as she ran. Several drones took notice and fired at Melonie. She hunched over and blindly fired back at them as she fled deeper into the chaos.

A drone rammed the butt of his rifle into Melonie's chest, knocking her on her back. Melonie sloppily threw three daggers at the drone as she tumbled backward and the daggers lodged themselves into the drone's face and chest before he could react. Another Ski'tal aimed his rifle at Melonie's face, but she fired her pistol first and watched as his head snapped back before he flopped to the ground.

Melonie picked herself up, switched to her UMP, and charged forward. Any Ski'tal in her way received reactive bursts from her submachine gun to the hips and legs. Bullets flew past Melonie as she ran, barely missing her.

"Melonie, over here!" she heard a female voice shout over the comms. She slowed her speed and looked to her left, where she spotted Sreda motioning her over.

"I hope you know what you're doing, Sreda!" Melonie changed course and sprinted towards her. Sreda threw out three orbs that shot out a sickly purple smoke as they rolled across the ground. The Ski'tal that stood in the area began to cough loudly as blood leaked from their mouths and eyes. Some of the Ski'tal actually began tearing their throats out to rid themselves of the pain.

"What's in those things?" Melonie muttered as she removed her hood.

"Neuro-agent. Don't worry. It only hurts Ski'tal." Sreda turned towards the ridge and ran. "Let's advance."

Melonie quickly reloaded her weapons as she followed closely behind Sreda. "I see that, but I don't think that really answered my question," she said.

Bria crouched down behind a rock next to Malachi and began picking off Ski'tal one by one. She glanced to her right and saw Sreda's purple neuro-agent puffing smoke into the air. "Sreda's got Melonie! Focus on covering them, Malachi!" Bria patted Malachi's shoulder and the pair shifted their focus to taking out the troops in Sreda and Melonie's way. "Soon as we have them, we're pullin' out!" Bria watched as Malachi worked the bolt-action on his rifle after each shot. "Jeez, man," Bria chuckled. "Didn't know my dad was missing his hunting rifle."

"The shit works though, doesn't it?" Malachi said.

Bria laughed loudly. "The shit works your wrist." Malachi dropped three humans in a row and looked at Bria.

She paused and nodded her head. "Okay, short stuff. I see you."

Malachi smiled as he aimed down the sights and continued his covering fire.

"I could use some help, brother!" Iskander and Ryze tussled in the dirt, trading blows. Iskander punched Ryze's masked face, and Ryze kneed Iskander in the gut, tossing him off.

"Brother?" Ryze asked with interest in his voice. "There's more than one Hacon?" Ryze transformed his arm into a machine gun and aimed it at the trio. "And they say Ski'tal breed fast." Ryze fired his machine gun as soon as Alastor stepped in front of Iskander. His shield took the brunt of the attack, giving Iskander enough time to arm himself with his ACR rifle and shoot at Ryze, piercing his abdomen. Ryze grunted as blood shot out from the wound. He deployed his wings, opened his arms, and flew at them, his enormous wingspan sweeping them off their feet. Ryze stopped suddenly, flinging them into the heat of the battle as a large explosion went off nearby.

"Ozzi, danger close!" Iskander yelled.

"Ah crap," Ozzi muttered over the comms. "Sorry!"

"Sorry?" Velanna hissed.

Alastor shot up and warped to Ryze. He swung his sword down over his head, but Ryze blocked the attack with his forearm. Ryze deployed his wrist blade and jammed Alastor's sword in between the blade and his forearm. Iskander slammed his fist into Ryze's abdomen. He grunted and punched Iskander in the face. Velanna shot Ryze in the face again with her shotgun and his head jerked back unnaturally, before slowly lifting back up to its normal position. Ryze changed his free hand to a rocket launcher and aimed it at Velanna. Iskander knocked Ryze's hand away and the rocket careened through the air, wildly corkscrewing and spinning through the sky. Iskander grabbed Ryze's head and yanked him around.

"Stop shooting at his face!" Alastor yelled as he struggled with Ryze. He could barely hold onto his sword. "His chest is his weak spot!"

"That would have been convenient to know earlier!" Velanna responded, loading more shells into her shotgun.

"I told you this was easier said than done!" Alastor grunted. He gave up on trying to get his sword back and drew his 1911 instead. He fired it at Ryze's chest, but the bullets ricocheted off and were sent into the mob of combatants, killing three random soldiers. "Shit," he muttered.

"I thought you said his chest was the weak spot!" Velanna dodged Ryze's attacks.

"Well, the inside area of his chest is!" Alastor reloaded his 1911. "All I know is headshots do *not* work."

Velanna fired her shotgun at Ryze's thigh, tearing a hole in his synthetic muscles. Ryze screamed and clamped a hand down over the wound. Iskander kicked Ryze in the gut, sending him sprawling to the ground. Alastor's sword dislodged from Ryze's arm and he quickly warped to retrieve it.

"Impressive," Ryze grunted, breathing heavily. "But futile."

Sreda and Melonie ran through the crowd of Dirt Hounds while Bria and Malachi continued taking out troops to clear their path. Sreda fired her submachine gun into the crowd, striking the heads of several humans. Melonie covered Sreda with her UMP as Ski'tal leapt over each other to claw at the Dirt Hounds. An explosion blew a huge gap in the mob and various body parts flew everywhere. "Arashi, you dumb sack of fuck! Watch your fire!" Sreda yelled.

"Move faster then, you half-wit!" Arashi spat back. "I'm trying my best, but thinning the herd only works if friendlies aren't *in* the fucking herd!"

Melonie slashed at the legs of a drone charging at Sreda. The drone fell to the ground face first and Melonie finished him off with a headshot from her UMP. Sreda pointed to a nearby wooden ladder. "Up!" she barked. Sreda covered Melonie with her submachine gun as she climbed the ladder.

"Bria, we're coming up on your location," Melonie said.

"Prepare for retreat, everyone!" Bria yelled, firing several sniper rounds. She ran to Ozzi, who was still in the turret and climbed up the Humvee. "Focus your attention on Ryze. Get 'em outta the fight ASAP!"

"I can do that." Ozzi smiled and wickedly glared at Ryze in the distance through his goggles. "Danger close, Alastor!" Ozzi said over the comms.

Iskander and Velanna faced the horde of Ski'tal charging towards them. Iskander placed a cylinder on the ground and a metal barricade deployed from the center, providing cover for both of them. "We'll keep them off of you, Alastor!" Iskander yelled, but Alastor was far too preoccupied to respond.

"Alastor, I thought you said there was a better way to end this," Ryze said. He shot out his wrist blade and swung down on Alastor.

"Trust me, this is definitely not what it looks like." Alastor blocked the attack with his sword. "For one, we weren't supposed to get caught."

"Then what does this look like?" Ryze's temper was beginning to grow. He kicked Alastor in the chest and sent him stumbling backwards. Ryze groaned and held his thigh, but threw a stab at Alastor with his blade.

"It's us stopping your assault!" Alastor extended his shield and slapped Ryze's arm away. He stabbed him, piercing his shoulder, and Ryze screamed as blood shot out from the injury. "I can't let you attack those innocent people in NVC!"

"I'm disappointed. You've learned nothing from The Vault." Ryze chopped down on Alastor's hand, breaking his grasp on the sword. He yanked it out of his shoulder and wielded it himself. "The only way to end this war is to cut off the head of the snake. The Council must be destroyed." Ryze slashed at Alastor with his own sword but he blocked it with his shield. "Civilian deaths will do nothing but weaken my already unstable leverage." Ryze continued to swing Alastor's sword carelessly throughout the air.

"Alastor!" Iskander yelled in a strained voice. Alastor ducked behind his shield and looked at his brother. The Dirt Hounds were pushing past Velanna and Iskander, forcing their way into the base. Alastor equipped his SCAR and aimed it at the cluster of humans. He fired several times, aiming for their heads to ensure that each shot ended in a dead Dirt Hound.

Ryze took notice as well and swung Alastor's sword, lobbing off the heads of several Hounds. He fired his machine gun into the swarm and a haze of red mist filled the air as each human target was gunned down, but the Dirt Hounds only continued to charge at their combatants. "Ryze, what the hell did you do to piss these guys off?" Alastor smashed his rifle into the skull of a Hound who got too close and his head cracked open as he fell backwards.

"Exist." Ryze switched his arm to the rocket launcher and fired three rounds into the midst of the attackers. A considerable amount of humans were blown up, and Iskander and Velanna were flung away from the force of the explosion. Dirt Hounds pushed aggressively towards Ryze, grabbing the arm that held Alastor's sword. Ryze tried to shake off the Hounds as he continued firing machine gun rounds into the clamoring mass, their bodies dropping limply to the dirt ground. In his frustration, Ryze tossed Alastor's sword over his head as he fought to break free.

Alastor warped into the air, catching his sword mid-flight, and warped back down to the ground to check on a dazed Iskander and Velanna. "Anyone need a medkit?" Alastor asked. Velanna silently stared at Alastor through the locks of her disheveled brown hair. Her eyes glared at him, sharper than knives. Velanna shook her head slowly.

"I'm fine, brother," Iskander said. "Just a bit shaken."

Alastor turned to look at Ryze, who was fiercely struggling to shake off the ruthless Hounds. He fired several rockets that shook the entire base upon detonating. "Legion, come to me!" Ryze called out. Legion troops came running to Ryze's aid, clashing with the Hounds. Alastor heard a thump from the ridge above and, suddenly, a grenade exploded against Ryze's chest, sending him through the large building behind him. Several Dirt Hounds blew up upon impact, sending human and Ski'tal viscera flying through the air. Alastor looked up at the ridge.

"Compliments to the chef," Alastor joked.

"Ain't no thing, Alastor," Ozzi chuckled back over the comms.

"Team A, Melonie's here," Bria said on the same channel. "We gotta roll out!"

"Guys, hang on tight." Alastor held out his hands to Velanna and Iskander. Iskander immediately clamped his massive hand down over Alastor's. Velanna reached for his hand, but he flinched instinctively and reached over to place his hand on Velanna's shoulder instead. Alastor looked up at the ridge where Bria and the rest of Team B stood, took a deep breath, and warped out of the battlefield.

Chapter 6

Alastor, Iskander, and Velanna reappeared next to their SUV. Alastor slumped over and collapsed against the door face first, his battle mask leaving a large dent in the metal. Melonie rushed to catch him, but his long arms and legs proved to be a considerable challenge for her to hold up. "Bria, get the back door!" Melonie grunted.

Bria rushed over to Melonie and opened the SUV's door for her. The two laid Alastor across the length of the backseat. Iskander stood up and Bria looked up at the towering Knight as he rubbed his head. "Malachi's ridin' back with you guys. I'll ride with Melonie and Alastor."

Iskander nodded and walked back to the Humvee with the rest of the team. Velanna waited silently, her vixen eyes staring at the Blur Havok team. Bria jumped into the driver's seat of the SUV and Melonie sat in the back seat, resting Alastor's head on her lap. Velanna sat shotgun again and looked straight ahead, her eyebrows sunk low as she folded her arms across her chest. Bria pushed the ignition button and, in the split second it took for the SUV to rev to life, watched the two enemy factions below rip each other apart before she yanked the SUV in reverse and drove away.

"What intel did you guys get?" Bria asked as she cruised through the streets of The Slums.

"I saw a glimpse of some kind of list," Melonie said as she stroked Alastor's dreadlocks. She reached behind his neck, pressed a button on the back of his battle mask, and watched as the mask retracted, revealing his gently parted lips. His face was covered in soot, blood splatters, and dirt. “Nothing else important, though,” she concluded. She lovingly rubbed Alastor’s cheek with her thumb as she cradled his head. Melonie looked up to see Velanna glaring at her, seething.

Bria grunted affirmatively. “Hope those Dirt Hound assholes don't cause any more trouble.”

“I did see something...” Melonie hesitated, “odd.” Bria looked at her in the rearview mirror. Melonie looked at Velanna who, by the grace of God, was no longer glaring at her. “We'll talk about it later.”

Bria glanced at Velanna, then back at Melonie in the mirror and silently nodded.

Alastor shifted, groaning as he grabbed his jaw. Melonie gasped and placed her hand over Alastor's as he held it against his cheek. He opened his eyes and smiled up at her loving face. “Hey, babe,” he said, groggily.

“Good to have ya back, bro!” Bria said excitedly. “Rescue mission was a complete success. No casualties, thanks to *moi*.”

“Aw, shit. Bria's hittin' us with the French words now,” Alastor laughed. “Good job, sis.” Alastor sat up straight, only to realize that Velanna was sitting in front of him, but she said nothing and continued to stare straight ahead. The tension in the vehicle suddenly felt smothering.

The car was silent except for the faint music that played from the SUV's speakers.

Bria let out a long whistle. "So..." She awkwardly chuckled. "You guys hear about that new movie? Weren't you talking about it, Alastor? I heard it's getting awesome reviews—"

"Tell them what you did, Alastor," Velanna said coldly.

"Oh boy," Bria muttered.

"Here we go," Alastor groaned.

"Or rather, what you *didn't* do."

"What's she talking about?" Melonie asked.

"Your precious boyfriend here was going to let Ryze kill me." Velanna whipped around and looked Melonie straight in the eye.

"Okay, look—" Alastor said.

"Look at what?" Velanna growled at Alastor. "I saw the look on your face. You wanted me dead!"

Bria tried desperately to defuse the argument. "Now, guys. How about we just—?"

"You don't know what I want," Alastor said seriously.

"I know enough, Jack. Okay? What I did to you to make you want me dead is beyond me." Velanna turned back around and folded her arms.

"You know what?" Alastor growled. He shot forward and positioned himself so he could get a good look at Velanna's face. "I've had it with your fuckin' nonsense! You ever think about why I could have the *slightest* possible desire to want you dead, you *abusive asshole*?"

"Abusive!" Velanna let out a hollow laugh. "The sex with her must be fantastic for you to throw me under the bus." Melonie turned a vivid shade of red and curled up in her seat.

"Whoa, whoa!" Bria exclaimed. "Everyone calm down now. Let's chill—"

"There you go again with your lies!" Alastor gripped the middle console, ripping the fabric clean off with his armored fingers. "How about, instead of gaslighting me and making me feel like a fuckin' crazy person, you take responsibility for all of your screw-ups and selfish-ass behavior for *once* in your life?"

Velanna turned and looked out of her window.

"Or is that too much for a con like you?" Alastor continued. "Like I said, when this mission is over, you fuck off back to whatever hole you crawled out of!" Alastor threw himself backwards into his seat and covered his face, breathing heavily as he tried to calm himself down. The car was painfully silent. Bria looked over at Velanna to see a stream of tears falling down her face and she quickly shot her attention back to the road. After a few seconds, she looked at Melonie in the rearview mirror, who was rubbing the base of Alastor's neck. Bria sighed and turned up the music.

Bria finally parked the SUV at the Bureau after a ride that seemed to last an eternity. "Blur Havok members, meet in the briefing room. Knights of Hacon are on standby," Bria said.

"Got it," Ozzi said over the comms. "On my way."

Velanna stepped out of the car first, acknowledging that she did not belong in either group. Bria looked at the couple in the back seat and nodded before getting out, leaving them alone.

Alastor looked at Melonie and let out a long sigh, his shoulders finally relaxing. "I'm sorry you had to see that, babe."

Melonie placed her hand on Alastor's face. "It's okay," she whispered. Her hands were trembling. She knew now was not the time to tell him how she felt. Melonie moved closer to Alastor and kissed his forehead. He wrapped his arms around Melonie's waist and placed his head against her chest. "It's okay, baby," she whispered again, rubbing the back of his head. Alastor let out a long sigh.

Ryze entered his chambers, limping severely. Small trails of cyan blood leaked from the various holes in his body and he was sore and aching. He felt a slight bump on his arm as a small table fell over. The table was entirely too short for him to knock over with just his arms and he looked down, noticing that his wrist blades were still deployed. He slowly retracted them, wincing as they slid inside his forearms.

Ryze looked up at the wall where a jagged black, purple, and teal blade hung. He moved his eyes to look at the stuffed doll on his shelf – the one that looked like Fel. He trudged to the shelf, delicately picked up the doll, and stared into its beaded eyes. He thought about what Alastor had said: *Sounds more like you're moving on. That's healthy.*

Am I? He questioned himself. Ryze examined the doll. He had taken pristine care of this toy simply because of its resemblance to Fel, just like he did with her blade. Ryze began to question the sentimentality of it all. He shook his head to rid the fog from his mind and tapped at the screen on his forearm.

"Yes, sir?" a female voice answered.

"Kazt," Ryze said with a groan. "I need your assistance."

A long, deep sigh came from Kazt. "How much material do I need to bring?"

"No limbs lost. Just holes." Ryze looked at his body, examining the porous wounds. "A significant amount of holes."

"I'm near Keine. It'll be a minute," Kazt huffed. It sounded like she was walking. "I miss having six legs."

Ryze's eyebrows sunk. "Why are you telling me this?"

"Well, I thought you'd like to talk about it."

"Talk about it?" Ryze sneered. "I am not your therapist."

"I'd think you're at least a friend," Kazt said. "I guess." She paused. "Maybe."

"What are you on about?" Ryze asked, becoming more and more irritated.

"Nothing," Kazt said sharply.

Ryze narrowed his eyes. "I'm going to go now."

Kazt's voice suddenly sounded disappointed. "Oh. Okay." She paused for a few seconds. "I'll be there in two hours."

"Good," Ryze said. "Meet me in the command center."

"Okay. Bye," Kazt said in a high-pitched voice. Ryze hung up, looked at the doll, and shook his head before placing it back on the shelf.

"This war is making me lose my mind."

Bria stood at the elevator, waiting for it to arrive. The doors slid open and she took a long, deep breath before letting out an anxious sigh. *Gotta face this sooner or later.* She stepped into the elevator and cracked her neck. *You're doing fine. It's cool. Better than last time.* She rubbed her face with her gloved hand, trying to calm herself.

Suddenly the doors opened and Velanna stepped into the elevator.

Fuck.

Bria's anxiety began to quickly escalate. Suddenly nervous, she slowly slid to her right to let Velanna in, continuing to cover her face. Velanna stepped in and turned to face the double doors as they slid closed, and they silently stood side by side. Bria wiped her hand off her face and sighed.

"I'm not contagious," Velanna said with a weak smile. She seemed to have recovered from her argument with Alastor. Bria sniffed and grunted in response. She shivered involuntarily, but kept her anxiety at bay.

"I saw that, by the way."

She tried to pretend that she wasn't frightened by Velanna, but the hair on Bria's neck rose. "Saw what?"

"Your anxiety. You were about to have an episode."

Bria awkwardly paused. She slowly crossed her arms defensively. "You don't know nothin'."

"I've seen things, been places."

"Uh-huh."

The two remained silent for a few moments before Velanna turned her head towards Bria. "I can see how much Alastor has influenced you."

"If you mean 'Alastor told me about you', then yeah, he did."

"Did he?" Velanna said, slightly intrigued. "What did he say?"

Bria slowly turned her head to look at Velanna. "After that shit-show in the car, I'm pretty sure you can figure out what he's told me."

Velanna chuckled, acting as if Alastor hadn't chewed her out just minutes before. "Fair enough. I've thought about what he said."

"Uh-huh."

"I've decided to do exactly what he wants me to do," Velanna said with a flair of sass.

"Uh-huh."

"He clearly likes this Melonie girl, so I'll just let him come back to me when she's out of the picture."

"You keep believin' that." Bria looked Velanna up and down as the elevator doors opened on her floor. "Shit sucks."

"What do you mean?" Velanna said, raising an eyebrow.

Bria stepped off of the elevator and her signature bravado swiftly returned. "If you weren't such a crazy bitch, I'd fuck the shit outta you."

"Flattering." The doors closed in front of Velanna's smirking face.

Bria made her way to the briefing room. Ozzi stood with his arms folded across his chest, large holograms of the files Melonie had downloaded hovering above the table. "Tell me you've got somethin' for us in there," Bria said.

Ozzi stroked his beard. "Shockingly, this gives us more information than I anticipated."

Bria raised her eyebrows. "Like what?"

"I've translated this document. Remember how the ratio of Blur Havok to Ski'tal troops used to be four to one?" Bria waited with bated breath. "The Legion now outnumber us three to two. Ryze has a count of 374,442 as of September 9th."

"That's today." Bria paused. "Oh." She pulled on the collar of her fatigues. "Well, that *is* somethin', I guess."

Alastor and Melonie walked into the room holding hands. "Before we get started – no stealth missions. They clearly do not work in our favor." Alastor let go of Melonie's hand and walked up to the table. He had wiped the dirt and blood off his face. "What's the scoop, Ozzi?" Alastor asked.

Ozzi cleared his throat. "Luck's on our side today. According to this document, The Nexus requires several relay stations throughout Valhalla to regulate millions of connections to each Ski'tal. Each station is manned by an Officer in the area."

"So we pick an Officer, pick a station, and start bussin' heads." Bria smiled.

Alastor narrowed his eyes and grinned. "And I've got the perfect candidate." He pointed to the fifth name on the list. Bria looked at the name and let out a hardy laugh.

"The Knights and I will handle the relay station. It'll be a quick in-and-out," Alastor said. "Everyone else will guard the outside and keep any trouble from coming in. I'm gonna go talk to the Knights." Alastor walked out of the briefing room.

"Looks like he's going to leave us with the crazed criminal, then..." Ozzi said quietly.

"So, Melonie." Bria folded her arms and faced Melonie, smiling. "Did you tell him?"

Melonie blushed and looked away. "No." Bria threw her hands into the air in disbelief.

"What's stopping you?" Ozzi asked.

"Everything," Melonie muttered. "Velanna, this war, my feelings – my mind."

Ozzi walked up to Melonie and placed his armored hand on her shoulder. "Look, Mel. I'm not a romantic guy. I'd rather spend my time matchmaking other people than myself." He pointed his finger at Melonie's chest. "But if there's one thing I know, is that that thing in your chest has never steered you wrong when it comes to Alastor."

Bria jumped back into the conversation. "Except that one time when you friend-zoned him. Not your best moment."

Ozzi snapped his attention to Bria. "You are not helping."

"Just sayin'," Bria mumbled.

Melonie sighed. "It's just so hard to find the right time to tell him."

Ozzi turned back to Melonie. "What did I say back in The Vault?"

"'Be more sure'."

"That shit still don't make sense," Bria said.

Ozzi ignored Bria. "The right time will come and you'll know it."

“Why isn't Alastor saying it first?” Melonie asked.

“Mel. This is *Alastor* we’re talking about. When has he ever been forthcoming about his feelings?” Ozzi said.

Alastor stepped out onto a balcony, where the Knights of Hacon waited. They hadn’t noticed him yet. Arashi and Iskander watched the sun as it began to set over Valhalla, Sreda sat on a stone bench nearby, intensely focused on the odd-sounding rhythm her synthetic fingers were making as she moved them, and Malachi was polishing his rifle.

“How are you holding up?” Iskander asked.

“Hell if I know. I just want this mission to be over so we can fuckin' be done with Roark.” Arashi said harshly.

“Don't rush it.” Iskander leaned over the banister and looked at his younger brother. “You may come to realize that that’s not what you want.”

“The religious old bastard deserves it.”

“I'm sorry you feel that way, Arashi.” Iskander hung his head and looked down at the drop below.

Alastor finally announced himself. “Hey guys,” he said sheepishly.

"Good work out there, brother," Iskander said. The rest of the Knights approached Alastor, ready for action. "What's the next move?"

"I've got that for you," Alastor raised a finger, "but I couldn't help overhearing – what were you guys talking about?" Sreda's eyes darted away from Alastor and her fingers began making that strange sound again.

Click. Tick, tick, tock.

Click. Tick, tick, tock.

Click. Tick, tick, tock.

"What is that? Why is she doing that?" Alastor asked. "Is she having a conniption?"

"No," Iskander said. "The opposite."

"She's nervous," Malachi said.

"The hell?" Alastor said. "The killer, neuro-toxin chuckin' sister of mine is nervous? About what?"

Iskander looked down but Arashi was more than happy to step in. "Roark's gonna die."

Alastor's heart dropped. The father he had just reclaimed was about to leave him. Again. "Wha—?" Alastor huffed, suddenly finding himself short of breath. "Why?"

Iskander sighed and held his head up. "His synthetic implants were created by him but they tax the body in ways that regulation grade implants do not." Iskander tried to keep his eyes on his brother, but the hurt expression on Alastor's face made it difficult to do so. "The number of lives he'll have to snuff out with his implants would push him beyond anything a human could withstand," Iskander finished. Sreda continued her nervous rhythm.

Click. Tick, tick, tock.

Click. Tick, tick, tock.

"Can hardly wait." Arashi smiled.

Alastor looked at Arashi sternly. "Why would you say that?"

"I could tell you, but you wouldn't believe me." Arashi placed his hands on his hips. "Roark isn't the man you think he is."

"No one believes you," Malachi said. "You just talk shit. It's all you do."

"Eat shit, little man. I know what I saw."

Sreda stopped moving her fingers and began to repeat something under her breath.

"What's she saying?" Alastor asked.

"Little Angel," Iskander said.

"Father called me that when I was a kid," Sreda said, speaking for the first time.

Alastor looked intensely at Sreda, then snapped to Iskander. "Call him," Alastor ordered.

Iskander's eyes widened. "I don't know if—"

"Call. Him," Alastor repeated curtly. Iskander sighed and tapped the screen on his forearm a few times. A hologram of Roark formed over Iskander's arm. "Yes, Iskander?" Roark asked.

"Dad, what the fuck?" Alastor yelled.

Iskander rotated the image of Roark to face Alastor. "I sense you have learned something new about the condition of the fight," Roark said with an air of omniscience.

"When were you gonna tell me that this was a suicide mission for you?" Alastor argued. "Another lie, dad? Really?"

Sreda began the rhythm on her hands again. *Click. Tick, tick, tock.*

"I did not lie. I omitted information for your benefit. I did not want emotions becoming inhibitions, Alastor."

"If you're not gonna see the end of this mission, then what's the point?"

Roark let out a long, slow sigh. "To secure a future for my children – for my Knights."

"Here goes the religious, hoodoo-voodoo..." Arashi said dismissively.

Click. Tick, tick, tock.

"The Blood of Hacon is sacred. We must ensure that our blood is passed down for generations."

"This conversation just took a wild turn," Alastor muttered.

Click. Tick, tick, tock.

"The Warrior's Blood, son. You have it. Your siblings have it. I have it."

"Okay, dad. This is getting weird."

Click. Tick, tick, tock.

"Iskander: The Defender. Arashi: The Storm. Sreda: The Heart. Malachi: The Messenger. And you, Alastor, are The Avenger. Your names were given to you for a reason."

Click. Tick, tick, tock.

"Alright, *stop*!" Alastor blurted out. Sreda jumped and stopped fidgeting with her fingers. "Enough of the weird, spiritual, tribal, prophecy shit! I get it. You want a safe future for us." Alastor's voice softened. "But I just wanted a dad."

Roark looked at his son silently and studied him with his eyes. "I understand, Alastor. I do not want to leave you or your siblings, but the Synthetics must be stopped. You and I both know that."

"Okay," Alastor huffed. He looked away from his father. "We'll get it done."

"Thank you, my children." Roark's hologram faded away.

Alastor's shoulders slumped. He looked like a wounded puppy. Iskander walked up to him and placed a hand on his shoulder. "Alastor," Iskander said. He looked up at Iskander. "We may lose our father, but we will not lose each other. I know it doesn't mean much since we just met, but that's what family is for."

Arashi wrapped his arm around Alastor's neck. "I don't like the old bastard, but I kinda like you," he said with a smile. "I give my siblings shit but, in the end, I love 'em. You're one of us, bro."

Sreda silently walked up to Alastor and hugged him around the waist. "I don't want this, either," she whispered sorrowfully. "I don't like it." Sreda hummed as she held on to Alastor.

Malachi held his sister and rubbed her shoulder in a loving, comforting way. "We're here for you, bro," Malachi said to Alastor. "We've got to look out for each other."

"I grew up an only child. I always wanted to know what this felt like." Alastor smiled and placed his hand over Iskander's. "I appreciate it, guys."

Velanna ran her French manicure nails along Alastor's back as he furiously typed on his computer, looking over his glasses at the bright, white screen. "Are you busy, Jack?" she asked.

Alastor looked up and readjusted his glasses. "Uh..." he stammered. "Not gonna lie, yes."
Velanna poked her lower lip out.

"It's just homework." Alastor warmly smiled. "You know I always make time for you. What's up?"

"Am I beautiful?"

Alastor's heart started racing. "Of course." He looked Velanna up and down. She looked harmless in her green oversized sweater and black leggings. "Why do you keep asking?"

Velanna avoided eye contact. "You know..."

"We've talked about this." Alastor removed his glasses. "That *secret* of yours is not you."

"But I can't help but feel so ugly knowing it's a part of me."

Alastor smiled and reached for his phone. "I know who you should talk to. Bria's great with self-esteem—"

Velanna hastily placed her hand on top of Alastor's and pushed down on it, not letting him move. "No. This stays between us," she said sternly. "*All* of our business stays between us."

"I'm not gonna tell her, I just—"

"Jack," Velanna said with venom in her voice. "*No.*"

"Okay, okay," Alastor said. "Touchy subject. I get it."

Velanna slowly let go of Alastor's hand and he, in turn, removed his hand from the phone. "Thank you," Velanna huffed.

Alastor smirked. "You know what?" He stood up and placed his hands on Velanna's waist. Velanna looked innocently into his eyes. "How about I show you how beautiful you are?"

Velanna sighed. "I can't get enough of you, you sly dog," she said, grinning.

Alastor planted his lips on Velanna's and the two began moving closer to the bed. Alastor picked Velanna up and threw her down on top of it. She giggled at his audacity as he climbed on top of her and began kissing her again. He could feel the energy and emotion passing between their lips. Alastor pulled away to look at Velanna.

"I feel you, Jack," Velanna said. She placed her arms over Alastor's shoulders. "You feel amazing."

Alastor leaned in. "I feel you, too," he whispered as he passionately kissed her.

Chapter 7

Alastor met up with Bria, Ozzi, and Melonie. "Are we ready to hit that relay station?" he asked.

"Hell yeah," Bria said.

"Awesome." Alastor looked at Melonie. "You alright, babe?"

"Yeah, I just—" Melonie saw Velanna and the Knights approaching. She felt like those coveted three words she wanted to tell Alastor were taken from her again. "I saw something weird in Ryze's room."

"Like what?" Ozzi asked.

"Ryze had a children's doll."

Bria laughed through her nose. "There's a kid in all of us, I guess."

"It looked like Fel," Melonie added. Alastor gulped. The failed mission at the Scar Base was not something he thought about often. Nor was it something he wanted to remember.

"Where do you think he got it?" Ozzi asked.

"The Vault," Alastor muttered. He covered his mouth and began nervously pacing. Melonie noticed and kept her eyes on him.

"What's the big deal? So what if Ryze likes to play with dolls," Bria asked innocently.

"Bria, Fel died defending The Nexus, remember?" Ozzi said.

Alastor stopped pacing. "She didn't just die. I *killed* her," he corrected, reliving the mission in his head. "When Ryze finds out we're making a run on The Nexus, he's gonna flip." Melonie rubbed his arm to comfort him.

"And that's *our* asses," Ozzi added.

Velanna joined the group. "Sounds like we need to mind our p's and q's, huh?"

"We're ready when you are, brother," Iskander said.

Alastor nodded at Iskander. "We rendezvous at Midland Dunes. Let's move out."

Two SUVs came to a halt on the sand as the sun began to set, turning the sky a radiant orange. The clouds that hovered over the beachgrass and palm trees were cotton candy pink. Alastor stepped out of the driver's side, his armored boot churning the sand. The cool breeze swept through his dreadlocks, making his ponytail sway back and forth.

The relay station was an old, abandoned school. There were no guards on patrol outside, but Alastor could bet money that the inside was heavily guarded. "Ozzi, Arashi, no heavy ordnance." He turned to look at them. "We're too close to Downtown NVC. Collateral could be bad."

Arashi groaned. "That's going to make things a bit harder."

"The Knights and I will tear through the relay station," Alastor said. The waning sun obscured his view and he squinted as he addressed the team. All he could see were the legs of everyone in the party. "We hit fast and we hit hard. Load up on ammo." Alastor walked to Bria and Ozzi and wrapped his arms around their shoulders. "Guys, do me a favor," Alastor whispered.

"I know, keep an eye on the evil girl," Ozzi guessed.

"Exactly," Alastor said. "As long as a pair of eyes are on her, she won't get stupid."

"I'll put her in the dirt if she *does*," Bria growled.

"Knew I could count on you guys." Alastor let his friends go and turned right into a waiting Melonie. She smiled. "Good luck, Alastor."

Alastor walked up to Melonie with that same, roguish smile he had given her after they had survived The Vault. "When I've got you on my mind, I don't need luck." He locked lips with Melonie.

Melonie wrapped her arms around Alastor's neck and let him love on her. She could feel Alastor smiling through the kiss and no words mattered to her at that moment. He broke the kiss. "Stay put, this'll only take a minute," he said in a deep, sensual purr. Alastor let go of Melonie and joined the rest of the Knights. She blushed as she fiddled with her hair. Alastor knew how to make her feel like a schoolgirl again.

"Get a room!" Ozzi jokingly yelled.

"If you're done tradin' spit over there, you're gonna wanna stock up, Mel," Bria said with a faint laugh. Melonie giggled and joined her fellow teammates. Alastor and Velanna glared at each other as they walked past one another.

"I'll be on my best behavior, I promise," Velanna said. "Lest I face the wrath of Bria's sexual preference," she giggled.

"Back to normal. Who would've thunk," Alastor grumbled. He didn't stop for one moment to entertain that woman. Alastor approached the Knights. "You guys ready to kick ass?"

"Ass won't be the only thing being kicked," Sreda said.

"That's the spirit, sis!" Alastor offered his fist to her. Sreda stared at the gesture and tilted her head. She looked up and smiled at Alastor. "Maybe next time." Alastor lowered his fist. "On me," he said, walking through the Knights. They all pulled a baton-like object from their waists, each one unfolding and extending to form their own weapons. Iskander's transformed into a claymore,

Sreda's became a one-handed ax, Arashi's changed into a katana, and Malachi's formed into a mace. Alastor watched their weapons transform, trying to hide his envy. "Where can I get one of those?" Alastor asked, barely holding back his admiration.

"We can make you one when this is all over!" Malachi said excitedly.

"Bet." Alastor unsheathed his sword and pointed it to the relay station. "Knights – attack!"

The Knights of Hacon charged the relay station and burst through the decrepit double doors of the old school. As Alastor suspected, several Ski'tal drones were in the hallway, unprepared for the slaughter that was about to come down on them.

Bria sat on the hood of one of the SUVs. Her eyes were glued to Velanna, who stood on a rock and stared at the school the Knights were laying siege to. Melonie sat in the driver's seat, playing with the lights and windshield wipers, waiting for something to happen. Ozzi was muttering some calculations to himself, but he still managed to keep his eyes trained on the mercenary.

Velanna turned to look at them. Bria placed her hand on the grip of her sniper rifle and Ozzi stopped muttering, frozen in place. Velanna smiled and turned her head back around.

"Ay," Bria whispered. "Ozzi." Ozzi raised his eyebrows and walked over to Bria. "She's playin' us," she murmured. "It's a long game for her."

"Well, yeah, I kinda figured, but what makes you say that?" Ozzi asked.

"I've seen this kinda shit before," Bria added. "She knows we're watchin' her. And she's waiting for us to stop."

Ozzi nodded. "So what do you think the winning conditions are for her?"

"That, I have no idea."

The Knights of Hacon stormed the sand-filled halls, slicing and bludgeoning anything in their way. Alastor pulled his SCAR from his back and gunned down the drones in front of him. Their bodies fell back and slumped against the empty red lockers. Iskander heard a group of Ski'tal approaching from down the hall and swung his massive claymore, bisecting three of the drone's heads. The rest stumbled backward as they watched their allies get mutilated, but Malachi drew his P90 submachine gun and hosed down the rest of the group. A few managed to escape into nearby classrooms, but three of them were not so fortunate.

Arashi stabbed a drone sneaking up on Sreda and finished him off with a burst from his M4 rifle. The blood from the drone's head exploded, coating the sand-covered tile floor in vivid green blood. "Where are we headed?" Arashi called out.

"Sreda, give us some eyes," Iskander said, cleaning his blade of Ski'tal guts.

Sreda ran to a nearby console. Her hand shot out several wires and attached themselves to every available input. "Information, information, information," she muttered, then suddenly gasped. "Two here!"

"Two *what*?" Alastor asked. He bashed a drone into the wall with his shield, splattering orange blood across the wall. Alastor turned his attention to a figure walking into the room. "What the shit?"

Velanna stood in the middle of the large room with a lifeless expression on her face.

"Velanna, get back to your position!" Iskander commanded. Alastor looked at Sreda. She was frozen, staring intensely at Velanna with large, uncanny eyes. Alastor gasped and poked a few buttons on the screen on his forearm.

Iskander walked up to Velanna with his claymore over his shoulder. "Velanna, that's an order!"

"Bria, come in," Alastor said.

"Yeah?" Bria whispered.

"Please tell me you have eyes on Velanna." Alastor didn't know which answer scared him more.

"Yeah, she hasn't moved once. Why?"

"Oh my God," Alastor muttered, realizing what the alternative was. "Iskander!" Alastor rushed to Iskander to stop him.

Bria stood up and hopped off of the SUV. "Ozzi, there's somethin' going on inside," she said.

"What's up?" Ozzi asked, arming himself with his AUG machine gun.

Melonie gasped. "Alastor?"

Velanna and Alastor stood side by side, laughing at something. Just as Melonie was about to confront him, Bria held her hand up, stopping her in her tracks. "This don't add up," she muttered. Bria aimed her sniper rifle at Velanna as Alastor placed his hand on the small of her back. "I figured," Bria said.

Bria pulled the trigger, planting a bullet in the back of Alastor's skull. His head flung forward, but not a single drop of blood shot out. He rubbed the back of his head and whipped around, evilly glaring at Bria as his battle mask slid into place. Velanna scattered away from Alastor, then looked at Bria. "What the hell are you doing?" Velanna yelled.

"Savin' your sorry fuckin' ass!" Bria yelled back, firing three more shots at Alastor. He walked through all three bullets without flinching. Ozzi gasped as Alastor's eyes began glowing purple, and he racked the charging handle of his AUG before unloading several rounds of ammunition into Fake Alastor. Fake Alastor stumbled as the bullets pushed him backwards. Melonie fired her UMP at him, hoping she was doing the right thing. He took a few bullets in the face, then blocked the rest with his hand, as if the bullets were a minor inconvenience.

After Melonie stopped firing, he looked directly at her. Looking into his eyes, it became perfectly clear – *that's not Alastor.*

Velanna looked at Iskander. Her teeth looked *too* white as they sparkled behind her evil grin. Iskander reached out to grab her arm, but he was too slow. She grabbed Iskander's hand and flipped the titan onto his back with ease. She twisted his arm and he grunted, wincing in pain. "What the hell, Velanna?" Iskander grabbed her shoulder, but she yanked it off and crushed three of his fingers in her hand.

Alastor swung his shield at Velanna, but she blocked it with her forearm without letting go of Iskander. She lifted Iskander up and swung his entire body like a bludgeon straight at Alastor. He tumbled back, hitting his head against the lockers as he drew his SCAR. Velanna jumped on top of him and pinned him down with an incredible amount of strength.

"I knew this bitch was crazy!" Arashi yelled.

"It's not her," Alastor said slowly, fear taking over him.

Velanna's eyes began to glow purple as her jaw separated down the middle of her chin. It receded into the back of her head and a long, slimy, cord-like tongue wildly flailed from her mouth, smacking Alastor across the face. The skin on her face and the hair on her head seemed to dissolve and a metal, insectoid face took its place. Her body changed and morphed before everyone's eyes, revealing a heap of wires. The jawless thing screeched at Alastor, its sharp teeth rising above his head as it unraveled a reel of synthetic muscle from within its chest and wrapped around Alastor's rifle, crushing it into pieces.

"This nigga is a Sleeper drone!" Alastor struggled underneath the hellish abomination. "Get it offa me!"

"Let's unload on this sack of shit!" Bria yelled. Fake Alastor broke out into a full-on sprint and rushed at Bria. He grabbed her by the throat and lifted her off the ground. Melonie threw a dagger into the side of Fake Alastor's head. He dropped Bria onto the SUV and turned to look at Melonie as his battle mask opened up, revealing a horrid amount of triangular teeth and slime. Velanna fired her shotgun into Alastor's back and he screeched loudly. His armor rearranged into a skeletal, lanky metal figure with a jawless face and several sharp appendages lurched out, trying to stab Velanna. She dodged the attack, rolling across the ground towards the rest of the team. Bria panted rapidly as she picked herself up. She continued to fire her M110 into the metal beast until she ran out of ammunition and the chamber locked open. Ozzi charged the thing and punched it where its face would have been.

Bria reloaded her rifle and glared at Velanna, who was trying to catch her breath. "Y'know..." Bria slid off the hood of the SUV. "The fact that you couldn't tell that *that* wasn't Alastor and you were *that close,* "Bria slapped the bolt release, chambering a round, "says a lot about you, ya fuckin' dumbass."

Iskander tried to rip the Sleeper drone off of Alastor, but it had its synthetic muscles wrapped around his limbs. Alastor was lifted off the ground as Iskander picked up the Sleeper. He wildly kicked his legs to try to break free and the metal abomination let out another ear-piercing screech. Arashi ran at the cluster of operatives and thrust his katana into the face of the Sleeper. Its face split in half but it wrapped its tongue around Arashi's katana, pulling his hands into the mess of synthetic wiring in its chest. "Oh my *God*!" Arashi screamed in horror.

"How in the shitting universe do we stop this thing?" Alastor yelled.

Sreda pulled her wires from the console with a loud snap before running into the chaos. She slammed the palm of her hand again and again into the side of the Sleeper's head. "Hold still, you fucking fuck!" The two halves of the Sleeper's head slapped back together and bit down on Sreda's arm, but she didn't even react.

Iskander clasped his hand around the Sleeper's head and slowly peeled its teeth off of Sreda. Somehow, it still had Arashi and Alastor entangled in the vines of its muscles. "Alastor, warp for God's sake!" Arashi yelled.

"All that's gonna do is bring the ugly thing with us!" Alastor struggled. "I'm guessing you don't want the Sleeper drone in a God damn to-go box, right?"

"Malachi, what are you—" Arashi turned to look at Malachi but a group of Ski'tal were engaging in a firefight with him. "Son of a bitch," Arashi whined.

Melonie re-cloaked and ran around the Sleeper drone. It had entangled Ozzi in its synthetic wiring and every time Ozzi ripped the wiring off of his armor, two more tendrils replaced the damaged one. Suddenly, The Sleeper's head was forcefully reeled back and several holes appeared in its face. It screeched wildly and wrapped its wires around an empty space behind its head. Melonie de-cloaked and grasped at the wires around her throat, gagging loudly, but she continued trying to stab the Sleeper with her dagger as it throttled her neck.

Bria sliced the wires with her combat knife and Melonie dropped to the sandy ground, rubbing her neck. Before Bria could retreat, the Sleeper grabbed her ankles and hoisted her upside down. "Alastor," Bria grunted over the comms. "I'm guessing you guys are dealin' with the same thing we are?"

"If I know God's sense of humor, of course we are," Alastor said, his voice pinched. "Jesus Christ!" he suddenly screamed.

Velanna fired her shotgun at the base of the Sleeper's neck, causing it to stumble around. It slammed Bria into the ground then pulled her back up. Bria spat out a lump of sand. "I'm also guessin' you don't know how to stop it yet," she said with an unusual level of calmness.

"W— We'll get back to you on that," Alastor stuttered.

Melonie sliced at the tendrils trapping Ozzi, creating sparks as the dagger scraped against his armor. Ozzi tore the rest of the wiring away and pummeled the Sleeper's face. The stab wounds inflicted by Melonie had significantly weakened the hull of the Sleeper's face, and each punch exposed more of the Sleeper's raw muscle. It caught Ozzi's fist with its tongue, simultaneously coating his face in slime. Ozzi let out a high-pitched scream in disgust.

"Sreda, please be my favorite sibling and tell me you've figured this out." Alastor fought against the wires again, futilely stretching the cords wrapped around him.

"Your favorite? Really?" Sreda's voice tightened with excitement.

"Uh..." Alastor stammered.

Sreda used her free hand to project a hologram of the Sleeper. The Sleeper in the hologram had its wires neatly stretched out in a singular braid. "There!" she yelled.

"Where?" Arashi snapped impatiently.

"The spine! It connects all of the muscles to the nervous system!"

Iskander continued to pull apart the tangle of cords. "And which one of these is the spine, Sreda?"

Alastor's face brightened. "Someone slice the wire that goes up into its head!" he ordered. Sreda swung her ax at the head of the Sleeper, but it grabbed her ax just like everything else.

"Malachi, are you done with those drones?" Iskander asked.

"Great, the one person who has a weapon that *doesn't* cut things," Arashi muttered.

Malachi slayed the last drone and ran over to the mess of metal. "Did you say something about cutting?"

"Grab my sword, Malachi!" Alastor yelled. "Go for the neck!" Malachi grabbed Alastor's sword from his waist but it immediately fell out of his hand. "Shit, what is this made out of?"

"C'mon man!" Arashi yelled. Arashi pulled his arm back to try and stab the Sleeper with his katana again, only for his hand to get wrapped around the handle of his sword.

"Do we need to trade places, Malachi?" Alastor said callously. The Sleeper wrapped its wires around Alastor's neck and arms and began to choke him. *"I feel like you're not taking this very seriously,"* Alastor said tightly.

"Shut up! I'm trying! Carry something lighter next time!" Malachi firmly gripped the sword and hoisted it over his shoulder. He slowly and deliberately slashed at the Sleeper, managing to cut through nearly half of the wires before embedding the blade into its spine. Half of the Sleeper's body shut down, freeing Alastor and Arashi. Arashi landed on his side with a grunt. "Finally!" he exclaimed. "Good job, man!"

Malachi dashed away from the Sleeper. "'Bout time I got some recognition."

"Alright, don't let it get to your head." Arashi picked up his katana and readied himself.

"Bria," Alastor panted, rubbing his neck. "You there?"

"Barely." The blood rushing to Bria's head made it nearly impossible to focus. She tried to aim her MP7, but she couldn't keep a bead on the Sleeper's web of wires.

"Cut the spine, Bria!" Alastor grunted over the comms.

"Ozzi, Mel," Bria slurred. "Cut spine..."

"Spine?" Ozzi asked. "Did the definition of spine change recently? I see no spine!"

"I'm on it!" Melonie jumped right into the wires and jammed her dagger under the Sleeper's head. The Sleeper fell to the ground, releasing Bria, who flopped face-first into the sand. The Sleeper made a gurgling sound as it twitched and convulsed on the ground. Ozzi stepped over it and slammed his fist through its lacerated face. He ripped out the drone's glowing, purple brain and watched as it faded to black. Ozzi turned back to Melonie with the brain in his palm. "Ryze may need another beta test." Ozzi smirked.

Melonie rolled Bria onto her back. "Anyone got some fruit?" Bria groaned. "Heard it helps with headaches."

Melonie let out a sigh of relief.

The Sleeper slammed Iskander onto the ground. Alastor warped to his shield and back to the Sleeper, smashing it into its head as Sreda yanked her ax free and swung it down on its frayed spine. The drone's head separated and Alastor flattened it under his shield.

Alastor panted, trying to catch his breath. "Lead the way, sis." He sheathed his sword as the Knights slowly began to recover from the battle. "I hope to God there aren't any more of those things in here."

“Didn't get to check.” Sreda swept the wires off her shoulder. “Best to stay watchful. This way.” She pointed down the hall. Iskander collapsed his claymore and placed the handle on his belt. “That entire ordeal puts things in perspective.”

Sreda lead her siblings down the hallway. “In here. The eatery,” she said, pointing to the ancient school's cafeteria. A single drone sat in the room, typing on a console. The ticking and clicking from his metal fingers as they poked each key were the only sounds in the wide-open room.

“Let me talk to him.” Alastor smirked and walked into the cafeteria. He approached the drone and cleared his throat.

The drone whipped around. “Oh no,” he said, his mandibles moving as he spoke. “Not *you* people.”

Alastor grinned widely. “Hi, Targ.”

Chapter 8

Ozzi and Melonie helped Bria up. "Fuck me, I'm gonna have nightmares about that," Bria groaned as she dusted the sand off of her. Melonie smiled warmly and helped brush off a few grains.

"I'll be keeping this." Ozzi held up the brain of the Sleeper drone. "I could make something useful with it."

"Uh, guys," Melonie said. "Where's Velanna?"

"Oh shit." Bria twirled around frantically but Velanna was nowhere to be found. "Oh *shit*!"

"It's been so long, Targ!" Alastor threw his hands into the air. "You look good, man! Mandibles looking clean, packing on a little bit of weight."

"How did you find me?" Targ's voice trembled. "You shouldn't know about this place."

"Doesn't matter, buddy!" Alastor wrapped his arm around Targ. "What matters is that we're back together. By the way, I meant to ask, did you enjoy that sandwich Melonie made?"

"Yes, actually. I—!" Targ pushed Alastor away. "Get off of me!"

"You know this drone?" Iskander asked.

"Yeah, bro." Alastor turned to the Knights. "We met Targ during The Vault Incident." He turned his head back to Targ and gave him a cheeky grin. "He helped us."

Targ folded his arms. "They interrogated me," he said in annoyance.

"I'd call it 'assisted relinquishment of pertinent information'," Alastor said.

"Where's The Nexus?" Sreda blurted out.

Targ's insectoid eyes narrowed. "You— you're making a huge mistake." He slowly backed up, his digitigrade legs carrying him away from the Knights.

"Why's that?" Iskander asked. "The Legion is going to strike the NVC Council in a matter of hours."

"We can't let that happen," Malachi added.

"You can't have access to the lives of millions of Ski'tal," Targ said severely. "I won't let you."

"Don't worry. We only want the Legion's lives," Arashi said with a wicked grin.

"This is a secret I will die with," Targ said sternly.

"That won't be necessary," a female voice said. Velanna dropped down on top of Targ and drove the heel of her boot into the back of his head. Targ lay face down, unmoving. Bria, Ozzi, and Melonie ran into the room. "There she is!" Bria panted.

"What the fuck are you doing?" Alastor yelled.

"Special orders from Roark." Velanna grinned as she tied up Targ's limp body. "Got them after we found out about the relay stations."

"*I* didn't hear about these orders," Iskander said as he fiercely approached Velanna.

"Like I said," Velanna tied the knot on the hogtied Targ, "he gave them to *me.*"

"Oof," Arashi mumbled. "Looks like you're not his most trusted anymore, huh?"

"Sreda, go ahead and get all the information from this terminal," Alastor said. Sreda jogged over to the console and attached it to the wires from her wrist. Alastor stroked his beard and huffed, trying to keep his temper controlled. "Velanna, why didn't you tell us about these orders?" he calmly asked.

"When a client has a request, I follow it to a T." Velanna picked and fluffed her hair.

"So, he told you not to tell us?" Iskander growled.

"Not in so many words."

Alastor looked at Iskander. "Your move," Alastor said with his arms open.

Iskander immediately called Roark, who appeared as a small hologram on Iskander's wrist. "Dad, what is this?" Iskander asked.

"The hired gun must have completed her objective." Roark raised an eyebrow. "Is that why you're calling?"

"Yes!" Iskander hissed. "Why didn't you tell us? Why didn't *she* tell us?"

"I feared that, due to the contentious nature of Velanna and Alastor's relationship, he would go against the directive."

"More lies!" Arashi bleated. "Awesome!" Malachi jabbed Arashi in the arm to shut him up. Iskander looked through the hologram at Alastor, but he was staring angrily at Roark. Iskander focused his eyes back on him. "Dad, why didn't you just tell us?"

"Are you questioning me, son?" Roark's voice deepened.

Iskander looked like he saw a ghost. "No, sir," he hesitantly responded.

"My decisions are made for specific reasons." Roark's voice softened but remained firm. "To disrespect me with such doubt makes me ponder your allegiance, Iskander."

Iskander silently stared at Roark. "Bring me the drone. The attack starts tonight." Roark's hologram dissolved.

Alastor watched as Iskander processed what had just happened and what the implications of Roark's choices were. He had only known Iskander for a day, but the look of defeat on his face was completely foreign. "Hey, Iskander. I—" Alastor started.

"Don't worry about it, brother." Iskander's eyes were glued to the ground. "Just— give me a minute," he stuttered.

"You know when Roark gets like that, it means he lost the argument, right?" Arashi whispered.

"Not now, man," Malachi said, being respectful of Iskander's feelings.

Alastor turned to Sreda. "How much longer, sis?"

Sreda kept her eyes on the console. "This will take a set. You can take a break."

Alastor gathered what Sreda meant and nodded before walking over to his friends. Velanna trained her eyes on him with that signature smile on her face but Alastor ignored her.

"Bro, I'm sorry," Bria gushed. "That weird wire-thing attacked us and we just lost track of—"

"Relax, Bria, you did your best," Alastor said. "Velanna's conniving and sneaky. I know how hard it is to keep tabs on her." He looked back at Velanna, who was chatting with Sreda as she worked. "And how hard it is to shake her off."

Velanna entered the apartment in a long trench coat. The kitchen was dimly lit and Velanna turned the lights off as she moved to the bedroom. She entered slowly to find Alastor lying in bed, reading something on his phone. "Jack?" she said, her voice wavering.

Alastor looked up. Velanna stood in front of the half-open door with a wide stance, as if she was about to run. "Oh, hey Velanna."

"What are you looking at?" Velanna asked softly.

"Just a silly conversation on some forum." Alastor locked his phone and placed it on his nightstand. "You alright?"

Velanna stepped in and closed the door behind her. She let out a long sigh. "Yeah, just–" She ran her fingers through her wavy brown hair and scratched her scalp. "Yeah."

"You look stressed," Alastor guessed. "Come lay down."

Velanna slowly moved to the small closet. She disrobed to her undergarments and placed her clothes on a hanger, trying to obscure the contents of her attire. She slid under the covers with Alastor and rolled into his open arms. She laid her head on his tank-top-covered chest and sighed. "What's on your mind?" Alastor asked, kissing her forehead.

Velanna stared straight ahead. "Nothing," she said flatly.

"I know 'nothing' usually means something." Alastor's voice deepened. "You *sure* you don't want to talk about it?"

Velanna looked up at Alastor with wide eyes and he looked back at her with a small smile. She teared up. "I quit my job."

"What?" Alastor said, concerned. "Why?"

"I'm sorry, I just couldn't anymore," Velanna whimpered. "I'm trying, Jack, I really am."

"What made you feel this way?"

"I felt helpless," she mumbled. "I felt like I had no control."

Alastor pursed his lips as he thought about what she said. "Well, when it comes to getting stuff done, I don't think you can ever have complete control."

"Yes, you can. If you try hard enough. I've done it before." Velanna felt Alastor gulp as she said that. "Don't worry, I'll still have my half of the rent," she said as she snuggled up to him.

"That's... good," Alastor muttered.

"Night, Jack," Velanna said. Her eyes slowly closed as she exhaled.

"Goodnight," Alastor said wearily. He reached to turn the light off and the room disappeared into pitch blackness.

Alastor sighed.

"Long day, huh?"

"Yeah." Alastor removed his hand from his face. The stress of the mission was beginning to affect him. He and Bria sat next to each other while Melonie and Ozzi chatted at a nearby cafeteria table. The rest of The Knights stood in a triangle, conversing with each other. Velanna was still talking to Sreda as she continued hacking into the console.

"Feeling the same way, bro," Bria chuckled. "Not much of the day left, though."

Alastor looked at Bria. Although he saw a woman, he was remembering an innocent sixteen-year-old child. He lovingly smiled at his sister by heart. "Hey, B."

"Yeah?" Bria said.

"I'm proud of you, man."

Bria groaned. “Nigga, don't get all sappy on me.”

“Well, nigga, stop making me so proud.” Alastor lightly shoved her. The two laughed together and let their joy linger for a moment.

“So, your dad's kind of a dick,” Bria said after a while. “At least he's here, right?”

“Not for long,” Alastor sighed.

“What do you mean?”

“When he jacks himself into The Nexus, it'll kill him.”

“Oh,” Bria said sadly. “That sucks, man.”

“I'm trying to accept it.” Alastor looked at his siblings. “How's your dad?” he asked.

Bria felt her heart squeeze. “I, uh... don't know.”

Alastor nodded. “You still think he hates you?”

“I honestly don't know.” She looked up as she thought about it. “He could.”

“I highly doubt it, Bria. He's all alone out there. You should check on him. He's gettin' kinda old, man.”

Bria hung her head and sighed. “Yeah, maybe after all this bullshit is done.”

Alastor rubbed her back in a circular motion. “Love you, sis.”

Bria warmly smiled back at Alastor. “Love you too.”

Melonie was bouncing her leg up and down as she sat at the cafeteria table, watching Alastor and Bria talk. “I've changed my mind. I can't say it.”

Ozzi pushed off the wall he was leaning on and stood up straight. “What? What about 'be more sure'?”

“That's the problem. I was never sure in the first place!” Melonie whined. “I'm not even sure about being alive anymore!”

“Hey, hey, hey!” Ozzi placed his hands on Melonie's arms. “Mel, breathe. You are saying *really* stupid things right now.” Ozzi looked deep into Melonie’s eyes. “And I need you to *stop*,” he said coldly.

Melonie took a deep breath and exhaled slowly. “Okay.”

“This is gonna eat at you until you do it, you hear me?”

Melonie pouted at Ozzi and didn't respond.

“Don't give me that look. I'm not Alastor.”

Melonie groaned. "Fine. Any advice?"

"Sack up."

Melonie cocked her head back at Ozzi's reply. "Excuse me?"

"Look, I've got nothing else, Mel. You know the kind of guy Alastor is and what he's been through. He's not gonna say it first. He wants to know you feel the same way before he puts himself on the line for you."

Melonie looked over at her boyfriend, smiling and laughing with Bria. She looked back at Ozzi.

"Go for it." Ozzi smiled.

Melonie smiled back and turned towards Alastor and Bria, who were both getting up to join the rest of the team. "Alastor!" Melonie called out.

Alastor motioned Bria to go ahead without him. "Yeah, babe?"

"I've got to tell you something," Melonie said. "About us."

"Oh, uh..." Alastor stammered. "This is not really the best time, Mel."

"Really?" Melonie's confidence began to waver. "Oh. I'm sorry."

"No. No, you're fine." Alastor held Melonie's cheek. "You know, shit with my dad and this whole Nexus business. Dance card's kinda full right now."

"I get it," Melonie said softly.

"Besides, I want to give you my full attention." Alastor leaned in and gently kissed Melonie's lips and she couldn't help but smile. "I want to hear everything you have to say and I don't want to rush you."

Melonie couldn't argue. She needed Alastor to pay close attention to what she had to say, and she didn't want to be pushed, interrupted, or shut down. "You know me so well." Melonie kissed Alastor back.

"Come!" Sreda called out. "It's ready!"

"C'mon babe. Let's get this done so we can celebrate with a night all to ourselves." Alastor smiled.

Sreda snatched her wires out of the console. "Verfallen Coast. Signal originates from there," she said as she turned to the rest of the team.

"Great," Iskander said. "We can double back, pick up Roark, regroup, and make the final push."

"Can't believe the Civil War is goin' to end today," Bria said with wide eyes.

"Peace in our time doesn't sound too far-fetched," Melonie said with a smile.

"One problem," Alastor pointed out. "There isn't a damn thing on Verfallen Coast."

"Sack-of-shit dearest must've wanted Targ to guide us to a specific location," Arashi said.

"Maybe there's a method to his madness," Velanna noted. Everyone stared at her with a scornful, disgusted look. "All I'm saying is that I understand how he operates." She shrugged in defense.

"Load Targ into the transport. We're headin' back to Roark," Alastor said.

Melonie sat shotgun as Bria drove. In the back seat, Sreda was thumbing through holograms projecting out of her palm while Arashi stared out of the window, watching the clouds above. Malachi had nodded off, his head leaning against the other window.

Melonie looked at Bria and gave her a motherly smile. Bria glanced at her and awkwardly laughed. "What? Gonna tell me you're proud of me too?"

"Well, yeah." Melonie giggled. "It seems like just yesterday Alastor was training you."

"I have the scars to prove it wasn't yesterday," Bria joked. "You never thought about leadin' a mission?"

"Oh God, no. You know that's not my thing. You seem like a natural, though."

"Nothing we've dealt with today is outside of my paygrade." Bria laughed.

"You guys are getting paid?" Arashi chimed in.

"Yeah, but not like we deserve, that's for sure," Bria said.

"Wow." Arashi stared at the back of Bria's headrest, trying to process what she said. "Roark doesn't pay us."

Sreda closed her palm, shutting off the hologram. "Money should not be your motive," she said haughtily.

"Ay, this ain't fairy tale land. Beans and bullets aren't free!"

"Beans and bullets?" Bria asked. "The hell does that mean?"

"It's an old phrase from the United States' Civil War," Melonie informed Bria. "It represents food and ammo for the troops in a war."

"Oh," Bria said. "I can get down with that. Sounds like a fun day at the range."

Alastor had his feet hanging out of the window as Ozzi drove. Velanna and Iskander sat in the back seat with an unconscious Targ leaning on Velanna. An opaque grey trail of liquid leaked from Targ's mouth and onto Velanna's armor. "Guys," Velanna groaned. "He's drooling on me—"

"No one cares," Alastor cut Velanna off sharply. "Hey, Ozzi," he said, quickly changing the subject, "if the war ends today, what do you think is next for us?"

"Probably police work. Valhalla may be somewhat developed, but it's still relatively young compared to other countries," Ozzi said. "There's still land that hasn't been colonized."

"Wonder what it was like here before the bombs," Alastor said.

"I heard there was this freakish monster that would jump on people, beat them up with their feet, and carry stuff in a sack on their stomach," Ozzi said. "They're all extinct now."

"Holy shit," Alastor muttered. "That sounds terrifying."

"Yeah." Ozzi shuttered. "They were called kangaroos."

"Stop making up nonsense." Iskander leaned forward. His weight shifted the car and Ozzi barely kept the SUV on the road. "There were no such things as kangaroos. Your silly behavior knows no limits."

"There were totally kangaroos here," Velanna added. "I've seen a picture of one."

"Now *that* we can agree on," Ozzi said.

Ryze stood in the command center of The Wolves' Den. The orange glow of the fireplace gave the room a rustic, primal aura. He looked at after-battle reports from his top men. "Nearly 2000 Dirt Hounds killed. And they just keep coming." Ryze sighed out of exhaustion. The battle had left Ryze drained. He looked at the wounds he sustained in the attack and began to wonder if peace between the humans and Ski'tal was possible. *If there are these many humans in Valhalla that hate the Ski'tal, then what hope is there? And how much of Blur Havok is fighting in this war because* they *hate the Ski'tal?* A knock came from the door. "Come in," Ryze said authoritatively.

A female drone entered the room. Her frame was anatomically similar to a human female's hourglass shape, but her diamond-shaped face had metallic plates that flexed to convey emotion. Her blue eyes studied Ryze closely. She placed a satchel full of metal plates, wires, and tools on the table near Ryze. "It's better than I thought," she said.

"Good to see you, Kazt." Ryze relaxed and sat down at the table. "You're right, it looks worse than it feels."

Kazt examined Ryze's arms. The holes from Alastor's sword had made serious gashes in his biceps and left shoulder. She placed her hand on Ryze's shoulder as she leaned in to examine the wound. "Won't need a full replacement, but you almost lost this one."

"Hopefully I won't need any more replacements. This war will be over soon. I have to push to the end."

Kazt let out a concerned groan. "What?" Ryze questioned.

"This war will get you killed," she said sternly. She cut the frayed synthetic muscle from Ryze's bicep.

He scoffed as he raised an eyebrow. "There are only two options: success or death. It is merely an occupational hazard."

"What's the point of fighting if you won't be around to enjoy the rewards?" Kazt said as she pulled at the spool of wire.

"Rewards that are not mine to reap yet. Rewards that are hypothetical. To go into battle with such reticence will ensure failure."

Kazt glared at Ryze as she furiously sewed synthetic muscle back into his arm. Ryze looked back at her with a blank expression. He grunted intermittently from the pinching sensation as she operated on him. "Is there something you wish to discuss?" he asked.

"Don't assume your rewards are hypothetical," Kazt said, her eyes focused on Ryze's arm. "And don't assume you won't have some reticence."

Ryze pursed his lips, thinking about what she said. "What are you implying?"

She walked around the table and rummaged through her bag. "Ryze, the only reason you continue this war is to avenge Fel." Ryze's heart ached at the mention of her name. "It's understandable," she quickly continued. "You loved her and that love is irreplaceable." Kazt pulled out a welding torch and some red metal plates. "But with time, you have to let her go." Ryze looked at Kazt, perplexed. He could not hide the emotional pain he was feeling at the thought of Fel.

"If there is an outcome where you make it out alive after the war is over," Kazt approached Ryze with her supplies, "what will your life be? Constantly reminiscing about a time that you can't get back to? Pining for a woman who is long dead?"

Ryze stared at Kazt. After an awkward few seconds, he averted his gaze because he didn't have an answer. His eyes had a sadness to them, and Kazt placed her hand on his armored forearm. He looked up at her and was met with a warm, understanding smile. "Now, hold still," Kazt said, lighting her torch. "This might sting."

The two SUVs arrived in the small hangar of The Blood's lair and the team disembarked from their vehicles. "Whoa, nice crib," Bria thought out loud. It was sleek and black, just like the main chamber.

"Father wants us to meet in the war room," Iskander said. "Go ahead, I'll go fetch him." He walked off in a different direction, carrying Targ.

Velanna led the way. Alastor and Melonie walked side-by-side, holding hands. Ozzi lowered his goggles and scanned the architecture of the lair as Bria and the rest of the Knights followed behind.

"Have a seat," Velanna said as she entered the war room. Computer terminals lined the perimeter of the room while dozens of monitors watched over the occupants. A gothic, black table with twisted and jagged stone edges was mounted to the floor in the middle of the room. It was covered with maps, diagrams, plans, and schematics. The team took seats around the sinister-looking table. Alastor and Melonie sat next to each other, Bria sat across from the couple, and the Knights filled in the remaining seats. Ozzi took interest in one of the terminals near the rear of the room. "May I?" he asked Sreda.

"Of course," Sreda said with a hesitant grin. "Everything is mission-related, anyways."

"Yes!" Ozzi giddily hopped onto a terminal and began typing, looking through files and documents.

"So, I'm going to meet your dad?" Melonie asked sheepishly.

"Not the most ideal way I wanted you to meet the folks," Alastor chuckled. "But it'll do."

A mechanical clanking came from the hallway. It sounded like a march and had a strict, regal tempo to it. The thumping of Iskander's footsteps quickly caught up to the sound of the mechanical churning. Ozzi was silently reading something on the terminal screen, muttering to himself. His eyebrows furrowed and he audibly gasped.

Roark entered the room with Iskander right behind him. He smiled at Alastor. "Son," he said warmly.

"Hey, dad." Alastor stood up. "Meet my friends – Ozzi and Bria."

"Sup." Bria gave him a relaxed, two-finger salute as she lazily sat back in her chair, but Ozzi did not respond.

"And this is Melonie, my girlfriend," Alastor said as he helped Melonie up.

Roark took Melonie's hand, holding her fingers, and lightly shook it. "The pleasure is mine, young lady." Roark looked up at Ozzi. "And you, sir?"

Ozzi swiftly spun around, looking visibly flustered. "Hello, sir. Name's Ozzi," he awkwardly spat out.

Roark nodded with a smile. "This is the moment we've been waiting for," he started. "We will end the Civil War in one fell swoop."

"About time," Arashi added.

"I'm proud of all of you," Roark said. "You came together despite your differences and your pasts to help

Valhalla when she needed you most." He narrowed his eyes. "Are you alright, Ozzi?"

Ozzi began to twitch. "Just have a little social anxiety. It's fine."

Roark looked at Ozzi oddly for a few seconds. "Anyways, Iskander and I will be making the final preparations. You may stay here, if you like, Alastor."

"Cool with me, dad." Alastor flopped back down in his chair. Roark and Iskander left the room and headed back in the direction they came from.

Alastor looked at Ozzi with a raised eyebrow. "You good, nigga?"

Bria glared at Ozzi. "No, he saw something." Bria sat up and pointed at Ozzi. "What did you see?"

The other Knights took interest and Ozzi interlocked his fingers, nervously looking at his audience. "Bria, remember when I said that the Ski'tal Legion had an approximate count of 374,442 in their forces?"

"Yeah?" Bria replied.

Ozzi gulped. He looked at Alastor, knowing he would be the one most disappointed with what he was about to say. "Roark has documented that his implants are calibrated to deliver a payload that will..." Ozzi paused and Alastor's eyebrows sank, "that will wipe out 3.7 million Ski'tal," he finished. "The entire population of Valhalla."

Chapter 9

"DAD!"

Alastor and the rest of Blur Havok strode through the ebony hallways, searching for Roark. Arashi, Sreda, and Malachi trailed after them while Velanna casually strolled behind the group.

"Why would he lie about this?" Melonie asked.

"Don't know, don't fuckin' care," Alastor hissed. "We're gonna set the record straight."

"This is gonna be good." Arashi rubbed his hands. Sreda began her compulsive rhythm.

Click. Tick, tick, tock.

Click. Tick, tick, tock.

Click. Tick, tick, tock.

"Now, Alastor, let's not do anything rash—" Malachi began.

"This the kinda shit you'd be on board with, Malachi?" Alastor barked. "Is genocide one of those things you'd do for dad?"

"I'm sure there's a perfectly good reason."

"No reason is going to be good enough," Alastor dismissively said.

"Alastor, I know you're mad, but maybe we can solve this calmly?" Bria said, trying to be the voice of reason.

"I have a feeling that won't be an option," Ozzi said.

The group made it to the main atrium, where Roark and Iskander were speaking in calm, hushed voices as Alastor stormed into the room. "Dad!" Alastor barked.

Roark jumped at the sound of Alastor's booming voice. "Why are you so angry, Alastor?"

"Don't play fuckin' dumb with me." Alastor shoved Iskander out of the way. "How long were you going to hide the body count of the Ski'tal? You didn't tell me you wanted *all* of them dead!"

"What?" Iskander asked in disbelief.

"Figures, you kept all of us out of the loop," Alastor said. "What else are you lying about?" He shoved Roark. "Are you even gonna die when you access The Nexus?"

"Watch your tone, boy." Roark's voice was intense and full of scorn as he brushed off his chest. "The secrecy was necessary."

"So it's true?" Ozzi asked. "You want to end all of those innocent lives?"

"Why not just the Legion?" Melonie asked.

"We put the Legion down, another damned group will rise to take its place," Roark said matter-of-factly. "If we rid this country of all of the Ski'tal, we can ensure that none of those *robots* will be a danger to any more humans."

"I can't let you do that, dad," Alastor said.

"You think you can stop plans that were put into motion before your birth?" Roark scoffed. He stepped closer to Alastor, looking down on him. "The empire I will foster in the name of the Hacon family will be prosperous. And it will not be stopped by my own son."

"Papa Hacon, don't do this..." Bria anxiously pleaded.

"No, dad," Alastor said. "We're taking you in."

"Knights, Velanna – assist Blur Havok in seeing the door. But bring me Alastor."

Velanna stepped in between the members of Blur Havok and Roark. The team watched as Arashi, Iskander, Sreda, and Malachi surrounded them, arming themselves with their weapons.

"Guys, what are you doing? Stop!" Ozzi pleaded.

"I'm sorry," Iskander said. His claymore unfurled in his hand. "It's for the good of Valhalla."

Arashi shook his head in shame. "Until Roark's gone, I'm not safe. None of us are. I'm sorry."

Malachi pulled the charging handle on his P90. "We don't wanna hurt you guys. Please don't fight back." Sreda averted her eyes from Alastor as she silently flicked her baton, activating her axe.

Alastor's battle mask clanked onto his face. "So this is how it's gonna be." He looked at Velanna, who softly smiled at him.

"Yes, Jack." Six, large pointed spikes grew from Velanna's back. "It's just business." They extended outwards, bending at the joints until the tips of each appendage made contact with the ground. The limbs continued to elongate, lifting Velanna into the air until she was hovering over Blur Havok. Her spider-like legs bent at three joints and the tips scratched against the carbon fiber floor.

"Oh my God," Melonie gasped.

"Blur Havok, defend yourselves!" Alastor ordered, unsheathing his sword.

The team scattered. Velanna thrust one of her spider legs at Alastor but he blocked it with his shield and the leg slid off, puncturing the floor. Alastor stomped on the joint and Velanna yelled out in pain. As she retracted her leg, Alastor swung his sword at the next one, but another one of her legs seemed to appear out of nowhere to block the attack. One of Velanna's spider legs reached around Alastor's head and poked the button on the base of his neck, removing his mask while another leg smacked against his unprotected face, sending him flying. "I wanna keep that face of yours in one piece, Jack," Velanna jested. "So be a nice little boy and let this happen." Genuine fear shone behind Alastor's eyes, but he reactivated his battle mask.

Bria fired her MP7 at Arashi. He dodged it and swiped his katana at Bria, ripping her fatigues and grazing her bicep. Bria tripped Arashi and held her submachine gun in his face, but Sreda suddenly appeared and smacked Bria with the broadside of her ax. She tumbled forward and Melonie quickly replaced her. She slashed at Sreda with her daggers, cutting the inside of her thigh. Sreda kneed Melonie in the gut before punching her in the face. Melonie staggered back, but before Sreda could approach, Ozzi swatted her away with his forearm, sending her flying across the room.

Iskander swung his claymore into the side of Ozzi's armor, embedding it deeply. He shoved his hand in Iskander's face and the claymore dropped to the floor as he pushed him off. Iskander stumbled backwards and fell on his back. A sniper shot hit Ozzi in the back, but simply ricocheted off and flew straight into the floor. Ozzi yanked the charging handle of his AUG rifle and aimed it at Malachi across the room. He unloaded his gun on him, sending out a flurry of bullets and forcing him to flee.

Alastor ducked, dodged, and blocked Velanna's barrage of spider legs. She cackled above him as she stabbed the floor repeatedly, trying to pin him down. "Jack, you are so much fun!" Alastor fought tooth and nail below, sweating profusely. He bashed a leg away, only for another one to nick him in the thigh. Alastor warped into the air and delivered a dropkick to Velanna's chest, sending her reeling back. Her spider legs accommodated for her, stopping her from hitting the wall she was about to crash into. Alastor warped to his father and swung down on Roark with his sword. Roark raised an open palm and Alastor's hands opened, flinging the sword over Roark's head. He punched Alastor in the stomach and backhanded him, sending him spinning away. "Know your place, boy," Roark sneered.

Bria pulled out her M110 and fired at Iskander. The bullet embedded itself into his armor but made no puncture wound. He shoulder-charged Bria and she toppled away from him, striking the wall and leaving a large dent. Iskander stood by, waiting for her to get up. "Stand down, Bria," he said. Suddenly, Ozzi tackled Iskander and began pummeling his face. Bria used her rifle to help herself up. "Thanks, Ozzi," she said, her voice shaking.

Melonie and Sreda swung their bladed weapons at each other, sparks flying as they clashed with one another. Melonie noticed Velanna scurrying towards the fight, her spider legs carrying her forward at an alarming speed. Velanna threw one of her legs forward and Melonie rolled out of the way, barely dodging the bladed limb. Sreda stumbled backwards and turned her attention on Alastor, who was still engaging Roark. "Alastor!" Melonie yelled.

Alastor whacked Roark in the cheek with a right hook. He heard Melonie's call and spied Sreda lurking. He quickly drew his 1911 and shot at the floor in front of her, making her hop around to dodge the bullets. Roark swept

Alastor's leg and shoved his clawed hands around his throat. "You should feel ashamed."

"For what?" Alastor grunted. He glanced at his sword on the floor. Alastor kicked his father in the chest, breaking Roark's grip on his throat and warped to his sword. He armed himself and ran at Roark, stabbing at him, but missing. "I didn't ask you to wake up one day and decide to slaughter a whole race!"

"It is a cleansing, boy!" Roark jabbed Alastor in the throat and kicked him in the shin. He fell to one knee and Roark grabbed him by his dreadlocked ponytail. "You think the rest of Valhalla thinks like you do? The silent majority will rise up if given the chance. You will see."

Ozzi threw Sreda across the room and into Roark's sleek black chair, breaking it into pieces. Malachi fired his P90 at Ozzi and, even though he covered his face, a bullet grazed his cheek. Bria fired a round into Malachi's leg and quickly closed the gap, smashing the butt of her rifle into his face and knocking him to the floor. "Get out while you can, kid."

Malachi swung his mace at Bria's legs, ripping more of her fatigues and tearing some of her synthetic skin. Bria screamed as she toppled to the floor. "You can't stop us!" Malachi declared. "I won't let–!" Ozzi scooped Malachi up and threw him into Arashi, who was quickly approaching, knocking them both down. Velanna stabbed Ozzi's right forearm with her spider leg, ripping into his armor and puncturing his arm. Ozzi yelled loudly as blood poured from the wound. "I thought you'd have fixed that by now." Velanna evilly grinned down at him. Bria fired a volley of bullets from her MP7 at Velanna and her spider legs haphazardly scurried her away.

Melonie rolled and dodged Iskander's massive fists as they pounded into the floor, making craters in the white carbon fiber. Melonie cloaked and stabbed Iskander in between the plates of his armor. He roared angrily and blindly grabbed Melonie before swinging her into the floor. The force of the slam caused Melonie to de-cloak. She struggled to break free from Iskander's grasp.

Alastor managed to take a moment from fighting Roark and looked over when he felt the massive vibration of Iskander's punches. He was reeling back to punch Melonie but Alastor extended his shield and threw it at Iskander. The shield hit him in the face and flew into the darkness. Iskander staggered backwards, covering his nose and Melonie scurried out of the crater Iskander's punches had made. Roark clawed at Alastor's head, ripping into his dreadlocks and leaving a gnarled wound on the left side of his face. Alastor's hair fell out of its ponytail and over his right eye. He growled and bashed the hilt of his sword into his father's face, knocking him down. Alastor stabbed both of Roark's digitigrade legs and he lunged towards the floor, holding his sword against Roark's neck.

"Stop them, dad!" Alastor commanded.

Roark struggled to turn his head but he spotted Melonie and reached his hand out. Melonie started to gag. Her limbs began to shake until they could no longer hold her up and she collapsed to the floor. "That won't be happening, boy," Roark said as he tortured Melonie.

Alastor looked over at her suffering on the floor. All of her synthetic implants and limbs were starting to shut down. She was gasping for air and rolling on the floor with what little organic muscles she had left. Alastor looked back at his father. "You fucking let her go, now!" Alastor yelled at the top of his lungs.

"Call off your team," Roark said coldly.

Alastor pushed the sword closer to his father's neck. The sound of the battle behind them faded away until it was just him, his father, and the sound of Melonie choking on her own saliva. "Please stop this, dad!" Alastor pleaded, his voice breaking in desperation.

"No," his father replied.

Alastor looked into Roark's aged eyes and something deep down told him that this man was his father by name only. And he would let Melonie die just to win. Alastor let out a primal scream at his father and raised the sword over his head before stabbing the floor next to Roark's face. He stood and pointed the sword away from his father. "Blur Havok, stand down," Alastor ordered.

Everyone froze in place and ceased fighting as Alastor and Roark stared at each other. Roark stopped torturing Melonie and her gagging stopped. Alastor could not believe that the man who lay in front of him was his father.

The silence of the room was suddenly pierced by the sound of Melonie's scream.

Alastor whipped around.

Velanna had skewered Melonie through the back with one of her spider legs, pinning her to the ground. She was kneeling beside Melonie and watching with a self-satisfied smile as Melonie groaned in pain. She winced as she tried to push Velanna off, but the end of her spider leg was impaled through the floor.

"Like I said, Jack." Velanna retracted all of her spider legs, freeing Melonie. Her grin was the most unholy Alastor had ever seen. "I play to win."

"Melonie?" Alastor muttered. "*Melonie!*" he screamed in horror. He drew his 1911 and fired at Velanna. She leapt through the air, her spider legs launching her upwards, and landed behind Roark. Alastor ignored Velanna and warped to Melonie.

"Knights, Velanna – move out, now," Roark said hastily. "Get the Synthetic and begin the assault." Iskander stared at Melonie, lying in a pool of her own blood. "Now, Iskander!" Roark yelled and Iskander quietly followed his father's order. Velanna stared at Alastor from the entrance to the hangar before the door automatically closed on her smile.

Bria and Ozzi looked over at Melonie and Alastor. "No..." Bria whispered to herself.

Alastor dropped to his knees and rolled Melonie over. A large, bloody hole was in the center of her chest. Gnarled scraps of synthetic implants were strewn throughout her wound and in the puddle of blood on the floor. She was breathing in short, strained bursts. Alastor's battle mask retracted and his eyes frantically scanned over her body. "You're gonna be okay, babe," Alastor quietly cooed. "I've got you. You're okay." Alastor reached for the medkit on his hip and ripped it open. A tourniquet, bandages, gauze, antibacterial wipes, and a trauma pad all spilled out onto the floor. His hands trembled as he reached for the supplies. He unrolled the gauze and ripped open the trauma pad.

Melonie lay on the floor, silently watching Alastor. His movements were frenzied and unbalanced, but she was calm. Everything was getting quiet. She felt sleepy as her energy began quickly leaving her body. She used as much of it as she could to place her hand on Alastor's. He stopped and looked at her with torment in his eyes. She could feel him shaking, but the sensation faded away. Melonie tried to smile, but she couldn't feel her face. *Now's the time...*

Alastor brought her up onto his thighs, pulling her closer. Melonie kept trying to take a breath, but they were becoming labored. She smiled weakly at her boyfriend. "Alastor..." she rasped. "Baby..."

"Yes, babe?" Alastor softly said, his voice quivering. Melonie's small, frail hand crept up from Alastor's hand to his cheek. "I lov—" she weakly attempted. Blood leaked from the corner of her smile and Alastor's heart sank.

"I love—"

A final breath escaped her lungs as the life was stolen from her eyes. Melonie's hand slid off of Alastor's face and her body fell limp.

Alastor gasped. “Melonie.” He gently shook her body, senselessly hoping that it would bring her back. “No, please don't—” He frantically scanned her body. “Please don’t do this to me, Mel,” he said, his voice breaking again. Alastor jabbed the armor on Melonie’s left chest plate with his finger and the LED menu faded on. Alastor poked the exclamation point. An error tone harshly buzzed from her armor. “Melonie? C’mon babe, please–” Alastor kept poking the exclamation point but the error tone repeated with each poke. “Come back!” he screamed. Tears fell from his eyes and mixed with the blood from his wound. “Melonie, *please*!”

The woman of his dreams was gone. Alastor's face contorted and he began to weep. He folded in on himself, resting his forehead against Melonie's and cradled her body tightly. He wailed over her unmoving body, sobbing uncontrollably. “I love you! Please don’t leave!” Alastor's vocal cords ripped apart as he begged and prayed to whatever deity he thought would listen. “Don’t leave me, Melonie!” Alastor said as he continued to cry.

Ozzi fell to his knees next to Alastor, clutching the bloody wound on his forearm. He stared at Melonie's body with pained eyes. “No...” Ozzi's voice broke. “No, no, no...”

Bria slowly walked up to the two men mourning over the body of their lifelong friend. She crouched down and placed her hand on Alastor's back. “Alastor.” Her voice was high pitched and soft, like a child’s. “I know this isn't the best time—" Alastor continued to sob, pleading incoherently. Bria cringed at the uncomfortable sound of his pain. "I'm sorry, I—" Alastor heaved and gasped as he continued to make bargains with no one, begging for Melonie's life.

Bria finally stopped fighting the tears and let them fall down her face. "We have to keep moving. Melonie wouldn't want us to stop." She leaned forward and tried to look into Alastor's eyes but his face was hidden behind a wall of dreadlocks. He had stopped begging and just the muffled sound of his weeping remained.

Ozzi met Bria's eyes. "Bria," he said softly, his voice shaking as tears ran down his face. "Just go. I've got him."

Bria felt a stab in her chest. She realized that she had no guidelines, no orders. An insurrection like no other was upon Valhalla and her team – the team that she had worked with to save humanity – was so racked with grief, that they were not able to help her. And one of her closest friends was now dead.

Bria stood up slowly. "I'm sorry, Alastor," she said before turning away.

The power and endurance of Alastor's crying seemed infinite as Bria made her way to the elevator. The sound of her brother in arms in agony unnerved her on a level she had never felt before. He was like a wolf mourning over his mate. She pushed the single button for the elevator and the doors silently opened. Bria looked back one last time at Alastor. He was crumpled over, defeated – a proud warrior no more.

Bria stepped into the elevator and the doors slid shut. As it rose to the surface, she leaned against the wall and slid to the floor. She began to lose her composure as she realized that the fate of Valhalla was all on her now. Her face twisted and she began to cry. Bria pounded her fist into the wall, shaking the elevator with each strike. The anxiety that usually gripped her in elevators was gone and she covered her face, allowing herself to mourn for the few seconds the ride would allow her.

For she knew that this war would not allow her another moment.

Chapter 10

"Human citizens of Valhalla. Alastor Hacon has betrayed you."

The citizens of New Valhalla City looked up as the sound of a disembodied voice boomed through the streets. The giant screens that watched the corridors of the city flickered and wavered. Everyone looked at their phones as the same distortion plagued their personal devices. Roark appeared on every screen.

"Alastor has decided to place the Synthetics, or 'Ski'tal' as he and the sympathizers call them, before *you* – his fellow humans."

Mason and a large group of Blur Havok members watched on a large screen in the mess hall of The Bureau. Many of them signaled their allies to come watch the broadcast.

"Blur Havok has failed you. Your Council has failed you. Your paragon of peace, Alastor Hacon, has failed you. Bria, Ozzi, Melonie – all have failed you."

Ryze sat on the bed in his personal quarters. He stared coldly at his tablet, listening to Roark's message.

"But now, The Blood of Hacon will enlighten you all with the cleansing of the Synthetic race by using their precious, coveted secret: The Nexus."

Ryze chucked the tablet across the room, obliterating it immediately upon impact. "Kazt, assemble the troops!" Ryze's eyes shifted into a flaming orange.

"Which ones, sir?" she replied over the comms.

"All of them!" Ryze screamed angrily. He ran his hands through his vibrant red hair, panting furiously as he paced back and forth.

"Come one, come all, if you want to take part in the sanctification of this land, cleansing the metallic weeds from our soil. The war ends at Verfallen Coast."

Mason stood in the crowd of Blur Havok members. "You're not goin' any-fuckin'-where!" someone yelled out, and Blur Havok troops suddenly began fighting one another.

"Fuckin' traitor!"

"Synthetic bot-bitch!"

"Racist piece of shit!"

"We're goin' to The Nexus!"

Mason ran towards the rebellion. Absolute bedlam had broken out in The Bureau and members lay on the ground, bleeding from various wounds on their faces.

"I await your response, Valhalla. I know I can count on your support."

The palm trees swayed in the stormy wind as Roark stepped out of the transport. His clawed, synthetic talons trailed through the sand of Verfallen Coast with authoritative clarity. The relaxing sound of waves crashing and seagulls cawing contrasted with the dark storm clouds that hovered over the coast's horizon, covering the ocean in an oppressive, black shadow.

Sreda stood next to Roark. “Father,” she said quietly.

“Yes, my Little Angel?” Roark crooned.

“I'm happy that your plan is coming close,” she said as she struggled to articulate her thoughts. “But what about Alastor?”

Roark let out a disappointed grunt. “I regret that the situation developed in such a way. But that is the price one pays for idealism.”

Velanna stepped out with Iskander, who was carrying Targ on his shoulder. Targ was conscious now and shackled with glowing blue cuffs. Iskander was quiet and brooding.

“What's eatin' you?” Velanna asked casually.

“Shut the fuck up,” Iskander hissed.

“Don't tell me that you actually cared about that shishkabobed little twerp?” Velanna asked incredulously. “She was in my way.”

Iskander glared at Velanna with murderous intent. "I would heed my advice if I were you."

"Doesn't matter. *You're not.* "Velanna sped up her walk to get to Roark. "So, what's the plan, boss-man?"

"The dissidents of Valhalla will fill the void that Blur Havok was to occupy in this phase," Roark replied. He watched Iskander approach with Targ, purposefully dragging his feet as Malachi walked past him.

"Ready to go, dad," Malachi said with mild enthusiasm.

"Excellent. You've grown quite a bit, my youngest." Roark smirked. "Continue your efforts and you may become quite the warrior.

Malachi grinned, but his glee was immediately tempered. "What will you do when Blur Havok tries to stop us?" Malachi asked.

"They would regret it," Roark scoffed. "An attempt to retake The Nexus would be foolish."

Velanna shook her head and tsked. "Not a good way to look at it," she said, foreboding in her voice. Roark glowered at Velanna as if she had spoken a hex. "To expect anything less than a measured response from Alastor," Velanna continued, smiling at the knowledge of how her ex-boyfriend was going to react, "*would be foolish*."

Bria ran through the double doors of The Bureau as pandemonium consumed their headquarters. "What the fuck?" she yelled.

"Bria!" Mason yelled from a banister above. A Blur Havok member held him by his arms while another ruthlessly punched him in the gut. Mason kicked his attacker and pushed off the floor, carrying both him and his attacker out of Bria's sight. Bria was bum-rushed by a member with a wooden chair but she punched her attacker in the face, knocking her out cold. "What's goin' on here, Mason?" she yelled. Static buzzed in her ear as Mason's voice came through.

"Whatever happened between you and The Blood," Mason panted, "has stirred the pot, ma'am! We've got defectors trying to take our assets to Verfallen Coast." He grunted like he had just taken a punch.

A large group of rebels ran at Bria with ill-intent in their eyes. She instinctively drew her MP7 and fired her gun at the charging dissenters. Their bodies dropped lifelessly as red liquid sprayed from their wounds. Bria gasped. These people were her troops just an hour ago. She gagged at the sight of their dead bodies. *God damn it.* She watched as Blur Havok members clashed in a large, ugly scuffle. Bria growled. "Any one of these idiots attack you, you put a bullet in 'em," she ordered. "If you're still with Blur Havok – weapons free!"

Mason ran down the stairs to Bria's left, firing his G17 pistol into a large crowd of defectors blocking his way. "Bria!" he yelled. "They're stealin' the gunships, ma'am!"

Mason reloaded his pistol and continued to fend off his attackers.

Bria sprinted towards the hangar. She shoved and shot anyone in her way that had the audacity to aim their weapons at her. She leapt over furniture and staggered enemies as she bolted to the hangar. A defector armed with a crowbar blocked the doors and, without hesitation, Bria slammed her fist into the traitor's forehead, crushing his skull and instantly flattening him on his back.

Bria burst through the doors. Gunships lifted off, taking hundreds of Blur Havok traitors to Verfallen Coast. Bria armed herself with her M110 and tried her best to pick off her targets. She shot a round into the cockpit of one of the fleeing gunships and the pilot's head exploded. His body fell against the controls and the gunship tilted forward. It crashed and burst into a ball of fire, illuminating the dark hangar with an intense glow.

Bria aimed at another gunship and fired twice into the engine. It spiraled out of control and struck a nearby wall, exploding into thousands of pieces. She aimed at another gunship and pulled the trigger – but the trigger didn't move. By the time Bria had reloaded her rifle, all of the gunships had taken off, leaving her alone with nothing but the crackling fire of the two explosions.

"Ma'am!" Mason ran into the room with a large group of Blur Havok troops, all battered and bruised, but still ready to fight. "The bloody traitors flew the coop."

Bria knelt down and pounded the metal hangar floor, letting out a loud scream. She panted, finally realizing that her body had been pushed harder than ever before. "First off, switch to frequency 125.49," Bria said as she slowly rose. She waited as all of the remaining Blur Havok troops followed her order. "Anyone not on this frequency is considered a fuckin' threat and *will* get a bullet." She shook her head, trying to calm herself and get her mind back on track. She was also hoping that this was all some bad dream.

"Now what, ma'am?" Mason asked.

"You got a head-count?"

"We're down by at least half," Mason said. "Haven't gotten a good check on the amount of casualties yet."

"So I'm guessin' the non-dickheads are here, right?"

"Safe to assume," Mason said.

"Okay." Bria tried to slow her breath. She was at a loss for ideas and plans. Alastor and Ozzi were still at The Blood's lair. She knew she only had one choice, but it was a stretch. She raised her wrist and made a call. The audible static in the call changed, letting her know that someone had answered. But there was no voice to greet her.

"This old frequency works. Color me shocked," Bria said. "You game for some crazy shit?"

Roark and the Knights of Hacon approached the edge of the ocean, letting the waves lap over their feet.

Roark walked to Iskander and yanked the cuffs off of Targ's ankles. "Put him down," Roark told him. Iskander stared at his father angrily and didn't move.

"My patience is wearing thin with you, Iskander," Roark growled. *"Put him down."*

Iskander dropped Targ and backed away, never breaking eye contact with Roark. Roark turned to face Targ, who was visibly shaken just by the sight of him. "Show us The Nexus," Roark ordered.

Targ looked at the Knights of Hacon. They all looked defeated and ashamed, but Velanna stared ominously at Targ with a soul-piercing gaze and a smile that sent shivers through his body. "I can't..." Targ murmured.

"Oh, but you can." Roark approached Targ with his hands behind his back. "And you *will.*" He placed his hand on Targ's head and his eyes flickered on and off like malfunctioning lights. Targ screamed, but his voice began to waver and distort. Roark pulled his hand away from Targ's head and leaned into his face. "Show us," he said, malice filling his voice. He pushed Targ towards the ocean and he stumbled forward before looking back at The Blood of Hacon. Velanna stood behind Roark and two of her spider legs rose from behind her back like scorpion tails. She stared at Targ with a wicked grin.

Targ turned back around and faced the clouds that hung over the deep blue sea. He stepped farther into the ocean and knelt down, placing his two-fingered hands into the water and activating an object outside of everyone's view. The ground began to rumble. Two black, metal towers broke the surface of the water and stretched into the dark sky, followed by an orange, hexagonal energy field. Encased within was a colossal, complex structure of stairs, walkways, and platforms in a honeycomb-like pattern. Roark stoically watched the foreign object rise from its watery grave.

The sound of trucks and aircrafts closed in on The Blood. Iskander turned to face the approaching force, looking in awe at the incoming army. Dirt Hound technicals, Blur Havok gunships, and forces from both factions walked towards them. They were all heavily armed and wore hardened faces that spoke for their ambition. A whole wall of them stormed the coast, ready to ally with Roark.

"Perfect. Valhalla never lets me down," Roark said smugly.

The dark, bronze encrusted chamber echoed with the frantic hissing and bickering between the five elders. The wooden pews that usually held an audience were empty and only a single, tungsten light illuminated the quintet. A guard in a black plate carrier, a burgundy compression shirt, black cargo pants, and black trainers stood quietly with her MPX carbine in hand. Her amber eyes scanned the room for any signs of danger. The door on the second floor of the chamber creaked open and the elders stopped talking. "'Turn the light on," the Hispanic female elder said. The guard slid up a dimmer on her right.

Bria stood front and center under the waxing spotlight. "Ms. Midgette," the Hispanic woman adjusted her black glasses. Her thin, sophisticated voice was scant of any bass, but she commanded with clear and unquestionable confidence and poise. "Luckily for you, Congress is not in session. You still have approximately two weeks left on your probation for foul language."

"Not the time, Vasquez," Bria said.

Vasquez raised an eyebrow and acknowledged Bria with a grunt. "I have no doubt Alastor Hacon and your team have this..." she held the sentence back trying to find the right word, "*situation* under control?" She turned back to her notes.

Bria stood strong but solemn. "No," she admitted. "I need the Council's help."

"Well, you haven't gone through the proper channels," Vasquez continued formally. "You must file a request through your Communications Officer, Melonie San—"

"Melonie's dead," Bria interrupted.

Vasquez fell silent. She covered her mouth and looked away from Bria. "Oh my... I—" she stammered.

"And Alastor is out of play," Bria continued. "Half of Blur Havok has committed treason and joined The Blood of Hacon."

Vasquez's formal political facade began to fail as she looked at Bria. "What do the numbers look like?"

"We're down by more than half."

"You don't stand a chance against them," Vasquez said, sounding defeated.

"That's why I need you to do something for me." Bria stepped to the side.

"She won't be alone." A pair of glowing green eyes cut through the shadows and a large, towering Ski'tal stood next to Bria. "My men are at the ready," Ryze said. The Council guard raised her carbine and aimed it at the Ski'tal as the Councilors began to panic at the sight of the Ski'tal warlord.

"What on God's green Earth is he doing here?" Vasquez gasped. "How could you bring him here?"

"He's here to help," Bria said. "And if you want this war to end the *right way*, you'll let him."

"Why should we trust him?" Vasquez spat back. "Your breeding facility plot was atrocious!"

"Because you need me," Ryze said. "As a sign of good faith and as an apology, let me show you something." Ryze snapped his fingers. "You two are dismissed." The two quieter Councilors stood up and morphed into Sleeper drones. Synthetic muscle unraveled from within the drones and the two Sleepers slithered away.

"Release the real Councilors on your way out," Ryze ordered. Vasquez was visibly shaken by the reveal, her eyes enlarged and dilated.

"If Roark wins, he will have an overwhelmingly murderous force at his command," Ryze said. "He will want you next and Blur Havok won't save you, The Ski'tal Legion won't save you, and your guards won't save you." The guard in the back of the chamber held her sights on Ryze. She trembled, but the darkness of the chamber saved her dignity.

"This is the best-case scenario, Vasquez," Bria said. "We honestly should've gotten chewed out for what happened in The Vault. We're tryin' to do it the right way this time."

"We have a real chance here, Councilor Vasquez," Ryze said with the utmost respect. "I know you and your fellow political elites hold resentment for my kind, but the only way to make relations better between our races is for you to authorize this alliance."

"Your call, Vasquez." Bria folded her arms.

Vasquez looked to her fellow Councilors on her left and right. Neither of them objected to the proposal, possibly out of fear of what Ryze would say, or because they genuinely saw no alternatives. She looked to the guard, who was still aiming her carbine at Ryze, and let out a long, concerned sigh. "Izabela, stand down," she told the guard. Izabela lowered her gun and sighed out of relief.

Vasquez turned back to Bria. "The Council motions to approve." Bria smirked, her confidence somewhat returning to her.

"On one condition – bring Roark and his associates in for trial," Vasquez said.

"With pleasure," Ryze said. Bria and Ryze turned and exited the chamber, leaving the rest of the Council dumbfounded.

Alastor dragged his feet.

The lifeless body of Melonie Sanders lay in his arms. His eyes were red and sunken as he stared blankly at her face. He appeared to have aged ten years in the span of a couple of hours. The blood from the wound on his head had dried into a dark red crust and his head pulsed violently.

All the memories of their life together ran through his mind: The time they snuck out on a school night to see the stars; when Melonie came over for dinner to meet his mother; that summer they spent together at his aunt's house, and when they went fishing and caught a huge catfish. He remembered the time they went to their first college football game, and when they shared their first kiss in The Vault.

"Alastor," Ozzi said, breaking his train of thought. They stood in front of the damaged Bureau. "Bria's taking care of whatever happened here. Come on," he said somberly as he slowly opened the wooden front doors of the citadel.

Alastor wordlessly stared at Ozzi before he dragged himself into The Bureau.

Ozzi closed the door behind them and scanned the vestibule, where dozens of bodies lay still and cold on the hardwood floor. Alastor continued to stare into Melonie's empty eyes, not once glancing up to see the aftermath of the treachery. His heart twisted as he searched for an inkling of life in Melonie's eyes.

Ozzi anxiously watched Alastor. "Let's go downstairs to the morgue," he said as he tried to bring Alastor back into their realm. He slowly turned his attention to Ozzi and they stared at each other for a few moments before Ozzi turned and walked through the corpses. Alastor never acknowledged the bodies of his men.

Ozzi pushed open a steel door and stepped into a cold, white room. Alastor plodded behind as Ozzi pulled the door open on one of the chambers and slid out a long metal tray. While he was dressing the tray with a body bag and all of the other necessary precautions, Alastor examined Melonie's limp body. Reality felt like a ruse, like someone was tricking him. He even questioned if he was really holding Melonie's corpse.

Ozzi cleared his throat and Alastor jolted as he was pulled away from his thoughts. He shivered as the cold air of the morgue finally hit him. The metal tray Ozzi prepared was waiting for Melonie, and Alastor placed her body inside the open bag. Ozzi sighed, his breath puffing from his lips as a warm cloud in the frigid air of the morgue. "You need rest," Ozzi said. "I'll handle this."

Alastor watched as Ozzi began removing Melonie's armor. "Wait," Alastor feebly said. Ozzi halted in his tracks. Melonie's static, cemented eyes stared at the ceiling. She still had the soft, bloodied smile she wore right before she died. Alastor let the armor around his hand peel back and he placed his gloved hand on Melonie's face, gently closing her eyelids. He looked at Ozzi and nodded.

Alastor stepped back as Ozzi efficiently removed the plates from Melonie's armor. Alastor paced through the morgue, looking at the name tags of all of the dead soldiers that awaited burial: Kyle T., Michael W., Travis L., Kasumi G., Jenna P., Will A., Helen E., Melonie S.

Alastor blinked quickly. The label for Melonie actually said "Miranda S". He was beginning to see things. Alastor exhaled and he felt his gut twist at the thought of seeing something so physical validate this nightmare. He sat on the frosted, tiled floor and watched as one of his best friends placed the love of his life in the dark, frozen prison of the morgue.

Alastor began to hear whispers, evil thoughts and memories of a life he wanted to abandon.

Without me... don't... nothing... only me... all mine...

Alastor tried to shake the thoughts that had haunted him all day, gnawing on his mind and prodding at his heart.

You're nothing without me.

Chapter 11

Ryze and Bria walked adjacent to each other as the remaining Blur Havok troops escorted them through the streets of New Valhalla City. As they approached the Slums, the quality of the buildings gradually degraded and Bria couldn't help but feel anxious; not for the coming battle, but because her father lived nearby in her childhood home. She wondered if she would ever see him again. She couldn't let this distract her.

Bria looked at Ryze. "Never thought we'd be on the same page."

"This is merely a mutually beneficial union," Ryze said. "You humans have a saying: 'The enemy of my enemy...'"

"'Is my friend'," Bria finished.

"I don't think that fits our situation quite yet," Ryze corrected. "Don't forget, you helped Roark access The Nexus."

"The bastard lied to us," Bria said shamefully. "If we had known his endgame, we wouldn't have helped him."

Ryze's eyes read Bria. She seemed genuinely ashamed of the betrayal and Ryze nodded, accepting her candor. "I digress. I am more concerned about what has my enemy scared enough to come running for help."

"Ryze, this ain't gonna cut it if you don't trust me," Bria said sternly. "I need you out there. I need you to trust me."

"You can count on me to operate at optimal efficiency." Ryze looked forward to the brewing storm. "But trust must be earned."

"If that's the case," Bria smiled, "I'm prepared to work for it." Ryze examined Bria. She was nearly half his size, but she had the vigor of a much larger soldier. He simply nodded, responding with an affirmative grunt.

Bria felt jitters. The circumstances sounded unreal. Her mentor was nowhere to be found but she was hoping that, at any moment, Alastor would appear and take charge. Each step they took towards The Slums made that outcome less likely.

A wall of Ski'tal waited at the city limits and Ryze raised his hand to his troops. The Ski'tal all looked relieved to see that their leader was back, but there was an odd energy in the air. Blur Havok and The Ski'tal Legion met and leered at each other – the two factions had only ever known the other as an enemy. The history between the two made the meeting awkward, but both parties could tell the other had good intentions.

"I hope you guys play nice," Bria said to everyone. "It's gonna be a long walk."

Roark watched The Nexus rise from the ocean. Water cascaded from the black structure and a long, narrow bridge began constructing itself from the base of the colossus. It snapped and clicked together as it traveled across the ocean, until finally stopping to lay flat against the coastal sand.

"Iskander, have you briefed the troops?" Roark asked his eldest son.

"Yes," Iskander growled.

"Good," Roark turned to Targ and raised his hand to him. "Open the door, drone."

"I must repeat, this is a grave mis—" Targ grunted as his eyes flickered again. He screamed out and fell to his hands and knees as a small stream of blood poured from his mouth.

Roark closed his fist and lowered it. "Next, I will ask my associate Velanna to assist in persuading you." Velanna walked up and stood next to Roark with a smug smile, staring down at the feeble Targ. "I would suggest making this easy on yourself," Roark added.

Targ coughed and blood sprayed from his mandibles, speckling the bleached sand with the purple fluid. He whimpered as he weakly stood up, holding his head with his cuffed hands. He muttered to himself incoherently as he walked towards The Nexus' broad front door.

Roark observed the black, clouded sky. "Iskander, get those gunships in the air to provide lighting," he said. Roark turned to Velanna. "I await this 'measured response'."

Alastor sat on the floor of the morgue and watched Ozzi zip Melonie's body bag closed. He slid the tray into the slot and closed the door behind it. Alastor looked at the pile of discarded plates, pieces, and Kevlar bodysuit that lay on the floor. It felt dehumanizing to see Melonie's armor like that. Alastor's sunken eyes stared at Ozzi as he completed the paperwork that would register Melonie into the database of casualties.

Ozzi slowly typed at the nearby terminal. He stopped and wearily sighed. "Should we notify her family?" he asked with a frail voice.

Alastor looked at Ozzi's back. He hadn't thought about that. What would Melonie's mother think? Her sister? He didn't know if they were even alive.

"Yes," Alastor quietly responded. Ozzi nodded and continued typing. The two occupied the room without any further conversation.

You're nothing without me... Alastor heard the whispers say. *Worthless.* Alastor felt the pull of the past tugging on his heart. He looked to the stark white lights above him as his heart weighed heavily in his chest.

His left thigh suddenly vibrated.

Alastor was sitting on the bed in his apartment. He pulled out his phone from his left pocket. A new text message from "B." Alastor unlocked his phone and read the screen.

yo thas fuckin wild nigga u gotta fix tht shit

The topic itself was not funny, but Alastor couldn't help but smile at Bria's lack of eloquence as he typed his response.

Yeah, not sure what to do. I told her that this is kind of a deal-breaker.

Velanna stepped into the room. She was taken aback by Alastor's presence and quickly shut her trench coat, tying it tightly. "Oh!" she exclaimed. "I didn't think you'd be here, Jack."

"Yeah, class was canceled today," Alastor said. He looked at Velanna's clothing and let out a long sigh. "Velanna, we need to talk."

"About what?"

Alastor stood up and brushed off his white t-shirt. "I think you know what."

Velanna folded her arms. "I really don't, Jack," she said with feigned laughter. It sounded more defensive than humoring. "Care to give me a hint?"

"It's about why you quit your job."

Velanna raised her eyebrow. "And?"

"And what you've been doing to make sure you have rent."

"I've been doing what I need to do."

"What's under the coat, Velanna?" Alastor asked with a sneer. "It's the middle of May and you're wearing a coat. You wanna explain that?"

"No, I don't," Velanna shot back. "Now leave it alone."

"I'm not leaving this one alone." Alastor stepped closer to Velanna. "What's under the coat?"

"Drop it, Jack," Velanna said darkly.

Alastor reached for the belt and snatched it. Velanna instantly grabbed the back of Alastor's mohawked hair and pulled him away, but her coat opened up. She was wearing a tank top with tight cargo pants, boots, and an operator's belt, complete with a pistol, spare magazines, and a combat knife.

Alastor winced as Velanna yanked on his hair. "There it is," he said, his voice strained.

"Shut it," Velanna hissed. "Jack Taylor. You think you're any better? I know your secret, *Alastor Hacon.* Why lie about something as simple as your name?"

"With a name like mine, connections are easy to follow."

"You think a name change would have saved you and your silly little clique, huh?" Velanna snarled at Alastor.

"My name is not as big of a deal as your criminal activity, Velanna."

Taking advantage of his chivalrous nature, Velanna pushed Alastor into the wall with a large thump that shook the entire apartment. "Listen, Jack. I do what I want, when I want. If I don't want some park-my-ass-in-a-desk job, then *I won't have it.*"

Alastor stared into Velanna's eyes. He had never seen her like this before. In no time at all, she had transformed into another person.

"I want control and life is easier for everyone when I have it. I need to know that I have everything under control," Velanna continued. "And god damn it, *that includes you.*"

Alastor felt a knot in his throat. He knew he had made a massive, irreversible mistake. "Velanna, this is not okay." Alastor's phone vibrated loudly enough for Velanna to hear it.

She bared her teeth and narrowed her eyes. "What did I tell you?"

Alastor remained silent. He felt a metal object slide into his palm and move his hand farther and farther up the wall. Alastor peered at his left hand to find Velanna's spider leg pressed against his palm. “Velanna, what are you—?” The leg pushed Alastor's hand and pinned it to the wall with its powerful tip. He grunted in pain.

“Our business stays between us,” Velanna growled. “Not Melonie, not Bria, not Ozzi, not your little circle of guy friends you met in college. Just us.” She tilted her head. “Why did you go behind my back? Why do you treat me so badly? Don't you trust me?” Velanna's face churned. “You make me feel so ugly. Making me use these *things*. I told you these things make me feel *ugly!*”

Alastor couldn't think of a response. All he could focus on was how much pain he was in as Velanna twisted her spider leg into his palm.

“So, from here on out, if I catch you going behind my back to talk to your little friends, I'll cut your hand off.” Velanna snatched her spider leg away, releasing Alastor's hand. He panted as he looked at his palm, which was leaking blood.

“Next time, just let sleeping beasts lie, Jack.” Velanna walked to the closet and began to remove her gear. “It'll spare you the cost of a synthetic hand.”

Alastor looked at Velanna with scorn and disappointment as she removed her equipment. “There won't be a next time,” he said, tears filling his eyes. Alastor began grabbing his toothbrush, soap, undergarments, and deodorant.

"Where do you think you're going?" Velanna said, watching him.

"Anywhere but here." Alastor continued to scan the apartment for items to take.

"You aren't going anywhere." Velanna stormed after Alastor. "No one wants you but me. Melonie didn't want you, remember? I'm the only one that wants you."

Alastor felt a sharp pain in his heart, but he continued to move, trying to ignore it.

"You hear me?" Velanna continued. "You are *nothing* without me! Worthless!"

Alastor felt like a dagger had pierced his heart, but he persevered, trying his best to ignore Velanna as he carelessly threw all the items in a sling bag and zipped it shut. He walked past her and towards the exit.

A spider leg planted itself into the door and Velanna slowly stepped in between it and Alastor. "You're not serious."

"I am," Alastor said. "Move."

"Just stay and talk about it."

"No, Velanna. I'm done with you."

"No, you're not." Velanna smiled. "You'll be back. You're all mine. I'm your drug, Alastor. I'll have you crawling on your hands and knees back to me, whether you know it or not."

Alastor fought back the tears that desperately wanted to escape. The relationship with Velanna had been an attempt to fill the void Melonie had left, which only exasperated the pain in Alastor's heart. He had foolishly tried to replace Melonie, only to find himself in a larger mess of emotions. "Fucking move, Velanna," he quietly said as the tears finally ran down his face.

Velanna gazed at Alastor. "Suit yourself." She stepped to the side. "You know I'm right."

Alastor flung the door open and flew down the stairs. Velanna smirked as she watched him flee.

"I told you, Jack."

The dark stormy skies covered Valhalla in a premature night as Velanna stood at the precipice of a platform on The Nexus, overlooking the army that protected her and her handler. The beachhead was a beautiful sight to her. All these men, stationed here and ready to fight. But there was one problem: They were not in her command. *Another bridge to cross at a later time.* The storm rumbled above her and she could feel the vibrations of the thunder shake through the metal beams of The Nexus. Velanna chuckled to herself.

"Come to me," she whispered into the ether. "You're all mine."

"How will we coordinate, Bria?" Ryze asked.

Blur Havok and The Ski'tal Legion began to approach Verfallen Coast. Bria could see the top of The Nexus and the flock of stolen Blur Havok gunships flying around the structure, protecting it. Their spotlights scanned the area for opposition.

"It's gonna be a hard push, not gonna front." Bria felt anxious as her face became damp in the cool evening weather. "We push hard, fast, and with no chill."

The sky let out a deep and foreboding grumble. The natural darkness of the night dimmed an already moonless horizon. Bria armed herself with her M110 rifle and turned to her men. "Guys, listen up," she said with wavering confidence. Ryze, Mason, and all of the troops behind them watched her in anticipation. Bria climbed a nearby rock to get a good look at their army. Thousands of humans and Ski'tal had come together for one cause – peace in their time.

Bria cleared her throat. "The odds look rough, that's just facts. But if we want this war to end with both sides happy, we need to fight side by side. Not as strangers, not even as friends. But as brothers." Bria looked down at Mason and Ryze. "As one," she finished. Mason smiled softly as Ryze nodded with approval. Kazt joined him at his side with an accepting grin.

"Now let's rock this shit!" Bria raised her rifle to the sky and all the troops called out, letting out an impassioned battle cry.

Alastor sat catatonically on the floor of the morgue. He was unsure if he lacked the will to get up or if he simply wanted to remain in that spot, rotting away in his mind. Ozzi was printing out files from the terminal he was working at. He reached towards the printer on his right but suddenly sucked in air. He looked down at his right arm and realized the large wound Velanna left had affected him worse than he thought.

Alastor looked back at the discarded pieces of Melonie's armor. He thought about how many times he had put his life on the line to save her. How hard he had fought to keep her from experiencing any pain.

How hard he had fought.

Alastor looked at his hands resting on his knees in front of him, his armored fingers hanging lazily over his shins. *What the fuck am I doing?* An insatiable rage-filled every fiber of Alastor's being and a raw, hellish energy filled his blood. It was like an animal had awoken inside of him. Alastor slammed his fist into the metal wall behind him, startling Ozzi. Alastor shot up and roared angrily as he swung around and ripped the large metal exit door off of its hinges, dropping it like a discarded plank of wood before stomping out of the morgue. Ozzi dropped the paperwork he was about to file and chased after his friend.

Alastor warped to the top of the stairs and stormed towards the front door of The Bureau while Ozzi scrambled to the top of the stairs as fast as he could. Alastor reloaded his 1911 as he strode towards the exit. "Alastor, stop!" Ozzi called out.

"No," Alastor barked as he pressed on.

Ozzi ran up to Alastor and held his shoulder down with his armored hand. "Alastor, wait!"

"*No!* "Alastor bellowed. He yanked his shoulder out of Ozzi's grasp and stared into his eyes. Ozzi was frozen.

Alastor's sunken eyes were a hazy, bloodshot red and the blood from his wound had coagulated over his left eye. He was a wounded wolf, baring his teeth and panting furiously in a defensive state. "I'm going to kill everyone who helped murder her! And if anyone gets in my way, they'll be in the dirt."

"You think you can just go out there and face an army alone?" Ozzi shot back. "I know you think you can, but you can't, Alastor."

"I can and I will!"

"I get it. You lost Melonie. But that doesn't give you a reason to throw yourself out there like an idiot!"

"You don't get it."

"Yes, I *fucking* do, Alastor!" Ozzi screamed at the top of his lungs. "Did you forget that I'm the one who had to put her back together after she tried to kill herself? The first piece of her body I found was her bloody charred jaw, ten feet away from her burning body as she screamed bloody murder. It took me *four days* to put her back together! Where were you when *that* happened?" Alastor stared at Ozzi, still fuming. "I haven't slept properly since I heard her screams," Ozzi continued, calming down slightly. "So yes, I get it." His voice broke as he started crying. "I get what it's like to put so much of yourself into someone, only for it to lead to nothing."

Alastor stared at his friend. He knew his callousness was uncalled for, but he had locked in his choice. "Then let's make sure that it doesn't lead to nothing."

Ozzi sniffed and nodded. "I've got just the thing," he said. "An asset from The Vault I've been waiting to use."

"Good," Alastor said, his voice rugged. "See you in the field." His battle mask covered his face as he warped away.

Roark stood on the second floor of The Nexus. The sea breeze kicked up, blowing the salty wind into the air. He heard a peculiar sound. "Continue unlocking The Nexus, drone." Roark walked away from Targ and stood next to Velanna. The sound grew louder – it was a low cry in the distance. Roark narrowed his eyes.

"Your measured response is here," Velanna teased.

Roark scoffed and dismissed the force as he walked away, sure that it would be taken care of. Velanna kept watch but she wasn't worried about it. She knew that the battle below would be a mere formality.

She knew Alastor wouldn't care about it either.

Bria and the squadron charged Verfallen Coast. Her face felt numb and cold but she felt the adrenaline coursing through her bloodstream as she focused in on every stimulus around her – the pounding of her military boots on the beach sand; the nylon texture of the strap of her rifle; the cool ocean air brushing against her cheeks. The Nexus slowly grew larger and a lot more real the closer she got – but they persisted.

The gunships above aimed their spotlights directly at the front line, lighting up Bria, Ryze, Mason, and Kazt. The bright white lights set the stage, the theatre of war that epitomized every conflict in the short history of this planet – but, still, they persisted.

Dirt Hound technicals revved up and drove through the sandy dunes, positioning themselves to suppress Bria's forces. Their former comrades scowled at them, the hate in their eyes finally visible. The whites of their teeth pierced through the dark night, practically ready to feast on their prey – but, still, they persisted.

The beachhead opened up, widening the already massive stage. Bria's world began to move in slow motion. The Dirt Hounds yelled and their turrets rotated as they warmed up, preparing to deliver a hail of fiery hot lead.

Only the large, gray rocks offered safety from the impending assault – but, still, they persisted.

This was it. The fight to end the Civil War.

The fight to end all fights.

The fight to avenge Melonie Sanders.

Chapter 12

"ATTACK!" Bria screamed, spit flying from her lips.

Dirt Hounds and Blur Havok traitors alike collapsed in a splash of red blood as a wall of bullets rained down on them. Ryze launched into the air and fired two rockets into the crowd of enemies, blowing groups of humans into pulpy, red chunks. "Push them back!" Bria bellowed. She fired into the crowd, downing three enemies. Dirt Hound technicals fired on the fellowship, splitting the heads both of Ski'tal and humans. Mason fired a 40mm grenade launcher at the technicals, blowing up one and forcing the others to flee. He continued to fire his grenade launcher at the trucks, blowing large spires of sand into the air with every missed shot.

"Ryze, we're gonna need cover as close to The Nexus as possible!" Bria yelled through the warfare. "Draw a line in the sand!"

"Affirmative." Ryze veered left of the fight and flew farther down the beach.

"Everyone, hunker down – danger close!" Bria yelled. She fired into the charging enemy as she crouched down to avoid the shrapnel. As bodies fell, the Dirt Hounds noticed what Ryze was doing and they started to scatter. Suddenly, the sound barrier cracked and a volley of rockets dropped from the sky, bombarding the Dirt Hounds. A large trench was formed in the wake of Ryze's bombing run.

"Go, go, go!" Bria yelled. "Push!" She fired her M110 through the waves of enemy soldiers. She looked up as a stream of bullets quickly traced up the beach, slicing into a portion of her men, and saw the gunships firing down on them. "Ryze, can you distract those gunships?" Bria asked over the comms.

"A tall order, but doable," he said calmly. Ryze fired rockets at the gunships, knocking them back in huge balls of fire. He flew past slowly enough for them to get a bead on him and half of the gunships split off to chase Ryze. "I'll double back and get the rest."

"What kind of rockets are those? They didn't do anything!" Bria yelled.

"They're anti-personnel, not anti-material, Bria," Ryze grunted, trying to dodge the gunship fire. "The scale of your assistance was greatly underestimated."

"What?" Bria fired her MP7 at the Dirt Hounds, thinning the herd.

"Worry about your lacking comprehension skills later!" Unease was beginning to creep into Ryze's voice as he continued to dodge the gunships.

Mason fired his grenade launcher straight into the chest of a Dirt Hound beyond the trench Ryze had made, and the human was blown to smithereens. Several of his fellow men were knocked back or gravely wounded. "Gun needs some more candy, ma'am. Where do I stock up?" he asked Bria.

“Go check with Kazt.” Bria threw her thumb over her shoulder. “Next person who speaks in anything other than English, we are fuckin' fightin'!” she crouched down and fired on the Dirt Hounds, pushing them farther back. They were almost ready to advance. The technicals returned and warmed up their turrets, before suddenly exploding right in front of Bria. She stumbled backwards, nearly dropping her rifle as several pillars of sand erupted into the air beyond the trench. Droves of Dirt Hounds burst open in a spray of red mist. Bria looked up and saw the gunships chasing after Ryze.

“Made another trench,” Ryze said, panting. “We are going to have to get rid of these gunships at some point.”

“God damn it. Next time, give us a heads up.” Bria reloaded her rifle and pointed forward. “Move up, everyone!”

Bria's squadron pushed up to the first row of trenches as bullets whizzed through the air, lobbing off chunks of sand from the lip. She spotted Roark and his Knights ascending the interweaving hexagonal staircases of The Nexus. Bria slid into the trench as Ski'tal and human alike continued dying, their bodies collapsing into the sand next to her. She panted as bullets flew over her head. Mason slid next to her with a reloaded grenade launcher.

“Mason.” She patted his chest. “I need you and a squad to suppress The Blood. Make sure they can't get to the top.”

“On it, ma'am,” Mason said, nodding. He pointed to a group of nearby Ski'tal and Blur Havok members. “You guys – get the bastards up there in the medieval clothes!" Mason and the squad fired at The Blood of Hacon. "Sit them down!" Mason yelled.

"Get down!" Sreda screamed. She pulled Roark away from the edge of the staircase as a hail of bullets and grenades hurtled towards the Knights. Velanna used her spider legs to carry herself onto the ceiling while Malachi and Arashi rushed away from the edge towards the hollow center as chunks of The Nexus were blown apart.

Roark, flustered, looked to Iskander. "Bring a platoon inside and cover our rear."

Iskander walked up to the edge, fully aware that the bullets were not likely to hit him at this range. "Troops – I need half of you to break off and cover our six," he said over the comms. "Do not let Blur Havok up here."

Ryze flew through the air, fighting frantically to dodge the gunships hot on his tail. He fired a volley of rockets behind him at his pursuers and one of them flew into the cockpit of one of the gunships and exploded, decimating the entire ship from within. "Danger close, humans!" Ryze warned. The smoldering remains spiraled down to the beach and crashed into the center of the battlefield, mowing down several Dirt Hounds.

Ryze latched onto another gunship. He dug his fingers into the glass and ripped the canopy off the gunship.

He jammed his wrist blade into the operator's head. Ryze detached himself and shifted into a nosedive as the pilotless gunship dove to the ground behind him and crashed in the ocean. He landed next to Kazt and fired his machine gun on nearby attackers. "Kazt, I need ammo," he said, breathing hard.

"Don't tell me you're tired already." Kazt smirked. She leaned out of cover from the rocks at the top of the beach to take potshots at the Dirt Hounds. "You sound like an old man trying to chase after his kids." She reached into her satchel and pulled out packets of ammunition.

Ryze grunted in disdain. His battle mask activated and covered his face. "Do not test me, woman." He snatched the ammunition from Kazt and flew away.

"Bria!" Mason yelled. "They're falling back!"

Bria peeked over the trenches and watched as Dirt Hounds fell back towards the entrance of The Nexus. A bullet flew at Bria's face and grazed her cheek. "Fuck!" Bria clasped her face and ducked down.

"Ma'am!" Mason called out.

A small stream of blood ran down Bria's cheek. "I'm straight," she sighed. "Only a scratch." She wiped the blood with her hand and onto her combat fatigues. "They're makin' a chokepoint and they're gonna keep us in place until it's too late." Bria looked to the black sky. "Ryze, we—!"

Bria heard Ryze grunt over the comms and she looked up to see his body hurtling uncontrollably towards the ground. He crashed into the coast, sending a swath of sand across the battlefield. Gunships hovered over the coast and sprayed down Blur Havok forces. "Mason, hit that bitch!" Bria ordered. Mason fired a grenade at the gunship and blew a hole in its hull. It began to smoke, but remained in the air, continuing to obliterate Blur Havok troops.

Ryze climbed out of the crater he had created, shaken but undamaged. "Enough!" he yelled as he fired hundreds of bullets at the gunships. Dirt Hounds focused their fire on Ryze, but the bullets bounced off of his body. Ryze pierced the cockpit of a gunship and turned the pilot into a red smear on the glass. The gunship rolled over into the ground and broke apart as its propellers churned into the sand, sending shrapnel and various parts of the ship flying through the battle. The last two gunships flew away to avoid Ryze. As he reloaded his machine gun, a rocket struck him in the chest, sending him flying backwards in a trail of black smoke. He tumbled in the sand until he fell into the trench next to Bria with a monstrous thud. "Damn it!" he cursed. His battle mask retracted as he clutched his chest. A large crack stretched across his breastplate and a small amount of cyan blood leaked from the crevices.

"Ryze, you're takin' an ass-kickin'." Bria rushed to him. "You need a patch up?"

"It's just the first layer," Ryze said, breathing heavily. "Besides, Kazt doesn't have enough time for a repair."

"The Blood is holed up in there," Mason intruded. "They're gonna starve us out of this fight if we don't break through into The Nexus."

"I can't take any more hits from those gunships," Ryze panted. "I'm grounded until they're down."

Bria thought to herself for a moment. "I got you." Bria pointed at the gunships above. "Your blue energy shit, you still have that?"

"Yes, but it is short-range and will knock my flight systems offline for a few moments."

"One shot's all we need." Bria turned to Mason. "Mason, lure those gunships closer with your 40 mike mike," she said excitedly.

"My 40 *what*?" Mason narrowed his eyes.

"The *grenades*, man! The *grenades*!" Bria hissed at him, shaking him back and forth. "Doesn't matter if they hit, just get their attention!"

Velanna watched the battle as she let her spider legs carry her up the stairs of The Nexus. Her heart beat excitedly knowing that Alastor would make his entrance at any second.

"Damn, what is up with the stairs?" Arashi asked. "Super advanced alien race and they ain't never heard of an elevator?"

"A defensive design choice I'm sure," Roark stated. "To delay the unauthorized from accessing what lies within. The key word being *delay*."

"Dad's always got the answers," Malachi said, basking in his father's greatness.

"You're such a brown-noser, I swear to God," Arashi jeered.

"At least I'm not a jackass loser," Malachi shot back.

"Oh, shut the hell up! I'm not the one kissing ass for cool points!" Arashi scoffed. "Can't even go seven seconds without sucking up to Roark, but *I'm* the loser?"

As the two brothers argued, Sreda began her signature compulsive sound.

Click. Tick, tick, tock.

Click. Tick, tick, tock.

Click. Tick, tick, tock.

"Worry not, my Little Angel," Roark said to his only daughter without looking at her. "Know that my actions guarantee a prosperous future for all of my children. Even those who are ungrateful."

"I don't answer to you anyway!" Malachi continued. "You ain't shit, you ain't never been shit, and you ain't ever gonna be shit!"

Velanna snickered.

"If you weren't my brother, I would beat the dogshit outta you," Arashi muttered, quelling the argument. "I care enough not to completely embarrass you."

"Aw, he cares," Velanna commented from behind.

"Shut up!" Malachi and Arashi yelled simultaneously.

"Nobody asked you," Malachi added with genuine disgust in his voice.

"Yeah, shouldn't you be committing crimes or something?" Arashi chimed in.

"I'm glad I can bring families together," Velanna chuckled.

"Alright, Mason," Bria pointed at the gunships, "let 'er rip!"

Mason fired grenades at the last two gunships in the air. They left a trail of light grey smoke and exploded in the air like crude, handmade fireworks. The shockwave of each discharge pushed and swayed the gunships like boats lost at sea and both flying death machines took aim at the trio on the ground, edging closer to ensure their rapid-fire guns were in optimal range.

"Herd 'em nice and close to each other," Bria told Mason.

Mason continued firing at the empty spaces near the gunships, forcing them closer to each other with each round. Ryze stayed in the trenches and kept the infantry at bay with his machine gun. Bria tapped Ryze. "Get ready, big boy. Fire when ready!"

Ryze looked to the sky at the encroaching gunships. They hovered right over the swarm of Dirt Hounds that blocked the entrance. He smiled wickedly as his right hand transformed into a machine that had a speaker-like device at the end. The energy disruptor hummed softly as it emanated a soft blue glow.

Mason fired two more grenades before the trigger clicked. "Guys, I'm out!" Mason yelled. "Reloading!"

Bria gasped and shot her gaze at the gunships. The turrets under the cockpit were beginning to spin. "Ryze?" Bria asked anxiously.

Ryze waited a few more seconds. "I have it," he calmly said. The propellers kicked up sand as the gunships crept closer, hovering over the coast.

"Ryze?" Bria asked again.

Ryze fired his disruptor at the pair of gunships. A wave of blue energy washed over the ships and the blades slowed to a halt as the force of the disruptor blast carried them towards The Nexus in a quiet arc. The giant hulls of the ships crushed the Dirt Hounds in their path and one of the gunships rolled to a stop on the bridge to The Nexus, its pilot killed in the impact of the crash. The other gunship lodged itself into the entrance.

"Mason, Ryze – light that ship up!" Bria ordered.

The pair fired rockets and grenades at the gunship lodged in the door. The overwhelming force of the explosions ripped the vehicles asunder, sending sheets of metal and chunks of mechanisms flying through the air as Dirt Hounds caught fire or lay on the ground with missing or gnarled limbs.

"We're rushing The Nexus!" Bria said over the comms. "Everyone, keep the fight down here!"

The cries of thousands of affirmations over the comms gave Bria the adrenaline rush of a lifetime. She finally felt like the leader she always wanted to be. "Let's fuckin' go!" she screamed ecstatically. Bria lead the charge past the crackling fires of the wreckage on the bridge to The Nexus. The metal bridge was a stark difference in terrain from the sandy beach of Verfallen Coast, the clunking of her leather boots on the metal floor echoing off the walls of The Nexus' interior hexagonal structure. A large column of green energy pulsed in the center of its chamber, stretching all the way to the top platform and a pair of stairs on both sides awaited the trio to send them up to Roark and his Knights.

"It all leads to the same spot," Ryze panted. "Just move."

Bria nodded and ran up the stairs to their left. "How long till your flight systems are up, Ryze?"

"That was a rather large blast." Ryze trailed Bria up the stairs. "It will definitely be a while."

"Fine. We high-tail it, then." Bria leapt up the stairs, skipping every other step to speed up the process. The stairs curved to the right as the trio scaled the honeycombed structure and the salty wind from the ocean kicked up and blew into Bria's face. She gasped and slowed her gait. A squad of Dirt Hounds stood in their way, armed with an assortment of weapons.

"I'm lettin' loose," Bria huffed.

"As am I," Ryze growled.

Velanna scurried behind Roark on her spider legs while Iskander trudged up the stairs with a scowl on his face. She looked at Sreda, who was not too far in front of her. Velanna decided to partake in her favorite past-time: stirring the pot. "Iskander, why the long face?" she asked. "Something on your mind?"

"Stow it, witch," Iskander barked.

"I don't think that was very nice," Velanna said with a condescending tone.

"Good," Iskander grunted.

Velanna moved around Iskander as they climbed the stairs. "I was just checking in on my new best friends," she said loudly as she watched Sreda from the corner of her eye. Sreda glanced behind her, then looked back around. Velanna seized the moment and scampered to Sreda with her insect legs. "Sreda," she said warmly. "We're best friends, right?"

Sreda gasped and slowed down, letting her father and Iskander continue without her. "I— uh..." she stuttered. "We are?"

"Of course!" Velanna said in a bubbly voice. "We're on the same team. And I know exactly how special you are, Sreda."

"You do?" Sreda's eyes widened. She began excitedly playing with her hair. "No one seems to have me."

"Oh, but I do." Velanna grinned devilishly, understanding exactly what Sreda meant. "Your mind – it's not like everyone else's. You think differently, right?"

Sreda's face lit up excitedly. "Whoa, you do know!"

"See?" Velanna leaned in closely. "And since we're best friends, I have a little secret I want to share with you.

It's about Alastor..." Sreda's expression grew more thrilled as Velanna leaned in and began whispering in her ear.

"Step aside or die!" Ryze's wrist blades shot out.

"Ryze, you know that's not happenin'," Bria said as she reloaded her MP7.

"I always like to give my opponents the opportunity to flee."

The Dirt Hounds rushed down the stairs and Bria fired her MP7. Three of them dropped to the floor and slid down the stairs, trailing blood behind them. Bria dodged an approaching Hound and kicked him in the back, sending him flying down the stairs in a heap of flailing limbs. Ryze charged and wildly swung his blades at them, slicing their small human bodies into messy halves. A Dirt Hound grabbed his arm and held it back, but Ryze turned to him and slammed his fist into the human's face, killing him instantly. Mason, armed with his assault rifle, lay back to provide clean-up assistance on any Hounds that got back up or managed to get past the two warriors. "Bria, Ryze, Mason – do you read me?" Kazt said over the comms.

"Yeah, loud 'n clear," Mason said, firing on the Hounds.

"A little preoccupied at the moment, what's up?" Bria panted. A Hound punched Bria in the gut and she jammed her combat knife into the collar of the Hound before throwing him over her head and down the stairs.

"Bad news. A wave of Hounds are on their way up The Nexus," Kazt said. "They pushed hard, I'm sorry."

"Affirmative," Ryze said. "I'll keep an eye on our six." He clobbered a Hound over the head, crushing his neck into itself.

Mason heard the impending Hounds on their rear. "Incoming, team!" He moved closer to Bria and Ryze and fired a grenade down the stairs, blowing up the front of the line of Hounds. The dead were immediately replaced with a new squad of leaders that charged through the mist of red blood. "That is definitely more than I thought," Mason said out loud.

"Shit, they're gonna sandwich our asses!" Bria looked at Ryze and smiled. "Heads up, Ryze!" Bria ran up to him and climbed up his back, perching between his wings.

"What are you doing, human?" Ryze chopped down on a Hound, embedding his wrist blade into her head. He ripped his blade out of her mutilated head and fired his machine gun up the stairs, flattening a bevy of Hounds, but more continued to rush down the stairs.

"Alastor told me something about 'the high ground'. Think he heard it from a movie." Bria held onto the collar of Ryze's armor and fired her M110 at the Hounds coming up the stairs. "Looks like it works!" Bria laughed. She continued to drop Hounds with headshot after headshot.

"Uh, Ryze?" Kazt said again over the comms. "I hate to have more bad news, but—"

"Oh shit," Bria gasped. A gunship rose from the ground outside of The Nexus, trailing smoke as it flew parallel to the stairs. Despite the wobbly flight path of the damaged gunship, it was quickly catching up to the team. "What the hell is that thing doing up and runnin'?"

"Shit." Ryze whirled around, nearly flinging Bria off of his back as he aimed his rocket launcher at the gunship. Just as Ryze was about to fire, the gunship exploded in a blast of electric blue energy, gore, and debris. Ryze grabbed Mason and threw him behind his back and Bria hopped off of Ryze's back, joining him. Ryze's armor shielded Bria and Mason from the inferno while The Hounds charging up the stairs were incinerated in the otherworldly combustion. All that remained was ash and flames.

A silhouette slowly strode up the stairs through the blaze, each step a strict, plodding march. The humanoid figure cleared the cloud of ash and stepped out, completely unscathed.

"Where is she?" Alastor Hacon growled from behind his battle mask.

Chapter 13

Bria stared at Alastor from behind Ryze. "Bro?" she softly said, confusion filling her voice.

"Alastor, I never thought I would be happy to see you," Ryze said, swinging off Dirt Hound remains.

"Roark and his team are headed up to the control room," Mason added.

"They'll be dead soon enough," Alastor growled deeply.

"What?" Bria muttered. "No, bro. Vasquez wants them alive!"

Alastor ignored Bria as he silently stared up the stairs, noticing the impending wave of Dirt Hounds. He unsheathed his sword and walked right past them as the Dirt Hounds ran down the stairs to meet Alastor. He cleanly sliced the heads off of the Hounds, and all seven of their bodies dropped at the same time, their heads rolling down the steps as Alastor marched up the stairs.

"What the fu–?" Bria watched Alastor move up the stairs like he was possessed. "Alastor?" she called out.

Alastor jammed his armored hand into the face of a Hound, impaling his taloned fingers into his face. He yanked his hand out and let the Hound's body drop to the floor. Another Hound ran at Alastor and he stabbed her with his sword before kicking her dying body off the ledge and into the ocean below. Alastor drew his 1911 and crammed his pistol into a Hound's mouth, breaking her teeth and forcing her to the floor. Alastor fired two rounds into the back of her throat before ripping the pistol from her mouth. He bludgeoned the bloody pistol against the jaw of another Hound and sliced his legs off with his sword. Alastor jammed his pistol into the Hound's eye and blasted a hole through the back of his head.

Bria ran after her best friend. "Alastor!" she called out again. He warped up the stairs, climbing the chamber rapidly with each warp.

"Ryze, please tell me your flight systems are up!" Bria turned to Ryze.

Ryze's wings let out a burst of flames and slightly lifted him off of the ground. "Good to go."

"We've gotta go after him," Bria said, pointing up the stairs. "Before he screws this whole thing up!"

Roark and the Knights reached a platform with a cylindrical pillar in the middle. "Drone, do whatever you need to do to navigate this chamber," Roark commanded. He shoved him towards a nearby panel and Targ slowly and weakly walked up to it, limping with each step. "Knights – secure the perimeter." Roark trailed behind Targ. "Velanna, stay mobile. Eyes open."

Velanna circled the platform on her spider legs as the Knights of Hacon spread out, patrolling the area for any suspicious activity. Roark watched Targ as he leaned against the panel and prepared to access it.

"How long will this take?" Roark asked.

"There are several safety mechanisms I must disarm. It will take time," Targ muttered.

"No tricks, Synthetic." Roark raised his hand to Targ. He nervously avoided eye contact and began working on the panel.

"Excellent. Keep at it, my childre—"

A thunderous whump came from the stairway and Roark looked up. "Knights!" he yelled. The Knights and Velanna converged in front of Roark and collectively gasped when they saw who their opponent was. Velanna immediately retracted her spider legs.

Alastor stood at the top of the stairwell with his sword embedded in the floor. His dark eyes stared wordlessly at his family and his ex-girlfriend.

"Son," Roark said. "I'm glad you could join us."

"Dad, stop," Iskander said.

"Shut your mouth, Iskander!" Roark scolded. "The boy needs to accept his damned place – and he will, whether he likes it or not."

"Let me talk to him," Iskander said. "Maybe I can spare us a fight."

Roark stared at his two eldest sons and nodded his head, silently obliging Iskander's request. Iskander stepped out from the group and walked towards Alastor. Arashi and Malachi looked at each other, unsure of what to prepare for. The popping of gunfire and the thumping of explosives was a quiet reminder to everyone on the platform that a battle was still raging below on the beach. Sreda looked back at her father, who was focused on Alastor and Iskander. Velanna waited with bated breath to see what would happen next.

Iskander slowly approached Alastor, who remained perfectly still. Anger radiated off of him. He spoke softly. "Alastor, I know you're upset about Melonie, but—"

Alastor leapt up and pounded his fist into Iskander's face, socking him in the jaw. He grabbed the back of Iskander's neck and slammed his face into the hilt of his sword before shoving his hulking body away from him. Iskander fell backwards and lay on the ground, his mouth hanging open. Alastor ferociously snatched his sword out of the floor.

"MELONIE IS DEAD!" Alastor screamed indignantly. He pointed the tip of his sword at the Knights of Hacon. *"And so are you."*

Alastor warped away and reappeared in the midst of the Knights. He raised his sword over his head and swung down on Velanna. One of her spider legs shot out from her back and caught Alastor's sword, genuinely shocked by his rage. He rammed his foot into Velanna's chest, sending her flying. Sreda swept her ax at her brother's legs, but Alastor grabbed the ax's haft and banged his forehead against the bridge of her nose. Sreda stumbled backwards, covering her nose with her hands. He dismissively discarded Sreda's axe as Arashi ran at him with his katana, but Alastor warped to the side and swiped Arashi's katana out of his hand. He grabbed Arashi's face and drove him to the floor. He struggled to get Alastor off of him, but Alastor raised Arashi's head off the ground and pounded it against the metal floor.

Iskander rushed Alastor and tackled him. Arashi rolled over and held the back of his head, groaning in pain. "Alastor, stop this madness!" Iskander pleaded. Alastor warped away and reappeared above Iskander, plunging the heel of his boot into his face. "We're your family! Plea—!" Alastor slammed another punch into Iskander's face, bouncing his head against the floor.

Alastor cocked back to unload another punch to Iskander's face, but he halted at the sound of Malachi's bolt action opening and closing. Alastor moved with blinding speed and lifted his sword to block the bullet, which struck the blade and fell to the floor. Alastor warped to Malachi and kneed him in the gut, sending him into the air. He grabbed him by the ankle before he flew too far out of reach and flung Malachi into the ground with an earth-shattering amount of force.

Arashi finally recovered and grabbed his katana. "Good goin', Velanna," he said. "Look what you've done!"

"A minor setback, I'm sure." Velanna leapt through the air at Alastor and thrust a pair of her spider legs into the floor, but she missed. "I have this under control."

Velanna frantically stabbed the floor as Alastor rolled, dodged, and warped to avoid her strikes. "Just hold still, Jack. I hate when you make me do this."

Alastor warped near one of the legs that supported Velanna and sliced at a joint. Velanna screamed in pain and fell on her back. He leapt into the air to deliver a killing stab to her face, only to be yanked back by some unnatural force. Velanna panted and patted her face as she picked herself up. Roark pulled Alastor out of midair with a chained blade planted into the armor on his back. He stepped out from behind the panel Targ was working on and yanked Alastor towards him, the chains reeling themselves in through a mechanism on Roark's forearm. "Your temper and unbridled recklessness will be the end of you, boy," Roark said calmly.

"And I'll be the end of you!" Alastor wildly rolled around on the floor, savagely clawing at the metal platform in a rash attempt to get back in the fight. In his fervor, the blade embedded in his back detached and, with two solid steps, Alastor shot up and rushed Roark with his sword. Alastor roared as he fiercely swiped at Roark, but his father gracefully dodged and blocked every attack. He suddenly threw a feint into the frenzy, and while Roark sidestepped a non-existent attack, it gave Alastor a moment to deliver a right hook to his father's face. Roark stumbled away and Alastor drew his 1911. He fired several rounds into Roark's legs, felling him to the ground. The 1911's slide locked open, but before Alastor could reload, Arashi grabbed his arm and held him back. Sreda joined Arashi and held onto Alastor's other arm. They dropped to the floor, forcing Alastor to fight against their dead weight.

"Alastor, stop!" Sreda pleaded. "Don't!"

"Just let the old bastard kill himself!" Arashi tried to reason. Alastor was pulling harder than Arashi thought he could. "We don't wanna fight!"

"I need you to stop, brother." Iskander placed both of his hands on Alastor's shoulders and pushed him down onto the floor. Malachi ran up and aimed his P90 at Alastor. He said nothing as a look of disappointment fell across his face.

Velanna sashayed towards Alastor. "This is a bad look for you, love," she joked.

Roark reeled in his blade, the chain clinking with each link that fed the mechanism on his forearm. "What a shame, Alastor," Roark strained as he slowly stood up. "The Warrior's Blood that runs through you is wasted on emotion and hopeless morals," Roark continued. He backhanded Alastor and fresh blood from Alastor's wound sprinkled over his face. "And you use them as an excuse to disrespect me when I *literally* want to give you the world."

Alastor's head rolled before looking up at his father with arched, angry eyebrows. "Melonie was my world," he said, his voice rough and damaged.

Roark finally saw the tears on Alastor's cheeks – he had been crying the entire fight.

"But you all took her from me," Alastor said with growing fury.

Mason stood in Ryze's hand, holding onto his shoulder, and Bria rode on his back as Ryze flew the trio up the thousands of stairs in pursuit of Alastor. "God, I know how Alastor gets, but this a new level. I've never seen him like this," Bria said to Ryze.

"I've seen that before," Ryze said, "in The Vault, when Alastor took my blade to save Melonie's life. The irreplaceable love that he had for Melonie..." he hesitated, even sounding slightly embarrassed. "Losing that would drive any man mad – human or Ski'tal."

Bria silently processed Ryze's words but she wasn't understanding the relevance.

"I read a quote once from human literature and it spoke to me," Ryze continued. "It said, 'those whom the gods would destroy they first drive mad'."

Bria's skin became cold and clammy. "Uh, Ryze? Why you tellin' me this?"

"I'm telling you so you know how to deal with it when this is over," Ryze said calmly. "Trust me."

Alastor strained to fight off his siblings, but they weighed him down with all of their might. Roark turned to Targ. "How much longer, robot?" he asked.

"A few moments," Targ replied, slowly maneuvering the panel.

Alastor pressed his knees away from the floor, using every human and synthetic muscle to fight against his siblings' strength. He managed to get the sole of one foot flat on the metal platform and Alastor shook violently as he rose. His inhuman strength flustered Iskander and he gasped as he tried to push harder against Alastor. Sreda dug the bladed tips of her legs into the floor, trying to stop him and Arashi stabbed the floor with his katana. Malachi backed away and lowered his gun, revealing his own bluff. Velanna's spider legs slowly grew out of her back as a look of surprise washed over her face. Alastor's arms shook wildly as Arashi's and Sreda's grips started to slip, and he howled loudly as he began to break his siblings' grasp on him.

Alastor ripped his hand out of Arashi's clutch and slammed the back of his armored forearm into his face, flinging him across the platform. He used his free hand to pound his metal fist into Sreda's face, knocking her into the ground. Alastor finally grabbed Iskander's large hands and slowly removed his grip from his shoulders before flipping him over his head, crushing Malachi underneath his weight.

Alastor quickly reloaded his 1911 and aimed it directly at Velanna. Roark raised his hand and shut down Alastor's implants in his right arm, making him drop the gun. Velanna smiled and drove a spider leg into his shoulder, ripping into his armor. Alastor screamed in pain, grabbing Velanna's insect implant. She closed the distance between the two and smugly chuckled. "It's just you and me now, Jack." She dragged her talons across the cheek of Alastor's battle mask. "In more ways than one." The Knights of Hacon had all recovered and were helping each other up.

Alastor grunted in pain. "You monster," he quietly seethed. The color red swarmed across his vision, painting the world in blood, as the hatred and anger consumed him. "What do you want from me?"

"You," Velanna said simply. "When I saw your handsome face all across the news as the new 'leader of Blur Havok', well, I simply couldn't wait any longer for you to come back to me." Velanna sighed dreamily. "The amount of damage we could do together, Jack," she looked at Roark, "after Papa Hacon's done," she looked back to Alastor. "We could have it all – manpower, weaponry, political control, Valhalla itself." Velanna's eyes dilated with excitement, high off the idea of control. "Queen and King, Bonnie and Clyde, Velanna and Alastor."

"You're crazy," Alastor said.

"Am I?" Velanna checked her armored nails. "I said you'd be back, right? That you'd come crawling back to me? Well, where are you now? May not be what we both thought, but I'm right all the same." She watched Alastor's eyes. They were hollow and sunken, but they stayed glued to her face. She could tell that he wasn't thinking deeply about what she was saying. "It will take time, but when there's only one option on the menu, you'll eventually eat it." Velanna narrowed her eyes and held Alastor's face in her palm. "And with a smile."

Alastor heard a familiar sound and Velanna gasped as she was suddenly sent flying backwards by the bullet in her chest. Her taloned spider leg ripped out of Alastor's shoulder and he fell to one knee, taking a moment to recover. He looked to his right as Ryze floated into view with Bria on his back and Mason on his shoulder. Bria held her M110 with an unflappable smile. "Sorry we're tardy to the party," Bria said. "We're bringin' you bitches in!" She and Mason hopped off of Ryze to engage the Knights of Hacon.

"Heathens!" Roark cursed from behind the panel. "Kill the humans and bring me the Synthetic in a can of parts!"

Ryze landed with a large thump, shaking the entire platform. He approached Alastor and picked him up off the floor. He looked Alastor in the eyes and saw through the facade of fury. "Fight hard, Hacon," Ryze said before running off to fight the Knights.

Iskander threw down a barricade. "Knights! Hunker down!" he ordered. He pulled out his ACR rifle and fired from behind his cover. Malachi rolled into Iskander's barricade, reloaded his rifle, and popped out to fire a round at Ryze. Ryze took the bullet to his masked face and walked right through it. Sreda leapt at Ryze with her battle axe, but he simply swatted her away. Ryze raised both of his bladed arms over his head to slice down on Iskander and Malachi, but Velanna blocked his arms with her spider legs, pulling him away. "Let go of me, you wench!" Ryze yelled.

"I will," Velanna grinned. "For the right price." An explosion flung Velanna and her mechanical legs flipping through the air. Mason reloaded his grenade launcher as her spider legs latched onto a horizontal beam above. She hung woozily, dazed from the relentless flipping. Bria aimed her rifle up at Velanna and prepared to fire, but Arashi kicked her in the back, knocking her to the floor.

"My bad," Arashi said. "Don't like hittin' a cute girl like you."

"When are you gonna get it?" Bria hopped up and slammed the stock of her sniper rifle into Arashi's gut. He collapsed to the floor, hugging his stomach. "I don't date dudes," Bria growled. "Fuck outta here." Bria raised her rifle and sniped Iskander in the back. Iskander stumbled forwards and turned to face Bria with a scowl. He began to charge at her, but before he could gather enough speed, Alastor warped in and slid into Iskander's shins, tripping him up mid-step.

Alastor kept his momentum and jumped into the air. He launched his fist towards Malachi, but he dodged the flying punch. Alastor drew his sword and swung at him, but Malachi sidestepped it and unfolded his mace. He bashed at Alastor's oblique with the spiked weapon and Alastor screamed out. He clawed at Malachi's face, tearing his olive skin and dying his face crimson. He slammed his fist onto the handle of the mace, flinging the weapon out of Malachi's hand, and punched him. Alastor followed Malachi to the floor, rapidly pummeling his face with his armored fist.

Arashi pulled Alastor off of Malachi, who lay on the ground, barely responsive. Arashi slashed Alastor's back with his katana and thrust it towards his thigh, but Alastor warped to his side and grabbed the arm that held the katana. Alastor twisted Arashi's arm in an unnatural direction, crumpling him to the ground. Alastor pried Arashi's katana from his hand and stabbed him in the shoulder with his own weapon. Before Arashi could cry out in pain, Alastor yanked the bloodied weapon from Arashi's shoulder and bolted towards Sreda. She and Ryze were locked in combat when Alastor took both Arashi's katana and his own sword and plunged the blades into Sreda's lower legs, pinning her to the floor. Sreda fell to her knees and feebly grabbed her thighs, trying to pull her legs free. She screamed hysterically, in pain, as she began to panic.

Velanna pounced on Alastor from above, her spider legs posing to strike, but Alastor yanked the two swords from Sreda's legs and blocked Velanna's attack. Iskander grabbed Alastor, but Ryze sliced his calf. He promptly released Alastor and Ryze tossed him over his head. Alastor threw Arashi's katana into one of Velanna's spider legs and she screeched as she scurried away.

Alastor prepared to fight Sreda, but she suddenly flew back and flopped onto her side, clutching her shoulder. Bria gave Alastor a thumbs up and reloaded her rifle. Iskander charged at Alastor and knocked him to the floor. He tumbled around for a few moments before digging his claws into the platform to regain control.

Alastor looked up to see Iskander rejoining Roark as his father forced Targ into a nearby elevator built into the central pillar. Velanna had recovered and was in the elevator with them. “You rat bastard!” Alastor roared. “Fight me!” He drew his 1911 and slung his arm up to aim at Roark.

“No!” a voice called out in desperation.

Alastor pulled the trigger and the .45 caliber bullet flew through the air. Roark stood in the elevator with a calm, aloof expression. As the bullet closed the distance, footsteps clanked on the hard metal floor and Malachi jumped through the air, directly into the path of the bullet. The hollow-point bullet pierced Malachi's forehead, splattering blood out of the back of his head. The blood sprayed onto Roark's face, startling him. He rubbed his hand across his face and checked to see what it was before he looked at his youngest son's unmoving body. Just like Malachi’s corpse, his face remained still. Iskander gasped loudly and looked at Roark’s lack of a reaction, but before anything else could happen, the elevator doors closed on the trio inside.

“Malachi?” Arashi crawled over to his younger brother. “No...” Arashi's voice broke. “God damn it, you little shit.” He strained to get up with his one working arm.

Sreda dropped to her knees and covered her head. Ryze was about to strike her, but he held back. Sreda began to mumble incoherently as she stared at Alastor, standing over Malachi's dead body. She tugged on her hair as the mumbling became complete gibberish.
Alastor stared down at Malachi’s face as blood started to seep from the back of his head, pooling behind him. Arashi slid as close to Alastor as he could get. “Now you see it,”

Arashi said. "What Roark really is." Alastor looked at Arashi with empty eyes.

"Would you believe me now if I told you he killed my mother?" Arashi said. "Right in front of my fuckin' eyes?" Alastor turned back to Malachi and knelt down, gently closing Malachi's eyes.

"That man was always evil. Malachi just never saw through it." Arashi rolled onto his bottom and sat in a defeated posture. "I only helped him because I can't stop him, Alastor."

Alastor looked up at the elevator doors.

"But *you* can."

Chapter 14

Alastor slammed his fingers into the crack of the elevator doors and yanked them open. He looked up the empty elevator shaft.

"Alastor, you can't go up there alone," Bria said. "We're goin' up there to finish this together."

Alastor didn't respond.

"I know this is how you roll, but Vasquez wants them alive," Bria said, trying to break through to him. "Besides, it's three versus one up there, man."

Alastor looked down the shaft, still not responding.

"Bro, c'mon don't—"

Alastor smashed his fist into the frame of the elevator, cutting Bria off. "I'm doing this alone." He glared at her, his hollow eyes loomed behind his dreadlocks. He looked completely unrecognizable. "This is all I have, Bria," he said quietly, his voice hoarse.

Bria stared at Alastor, remembering The Vault. It was the same look he had given her when he went to face Ryze alone, but this time, it was shrouded in a perverted, catastrophic veil. She knew he was going to have his way. "Okay, Alastor," Bria said softly. "But you better make it out of there alive." She turned to Ryze and Mason. "Arrest those two Knights and bring Malachi's body. We're gonna clear out those Hounds."

Ryze glared at Alastor. His green eyes told everyone on the platform that he understood what Alastor was experiencing. As much as he wanted to object and make sure The Nexus was secure, he acknowledged that Alastor was inconsolable. He grabbed a catatonic Sreda by the collar and lifted her off the floor as Mason picked up Malachi's body, throwing it over his shoulder. Bria hoisted Arashi up by his uninjured arm and walked him towards the stairs.

Alastor turned back to the empty shaft and jumped in. He dug his fingers into the walls and warped up the shaft.

The elevator doors opened and Roark, Targ, Velanna, and Iskander stepped out. They had reached a dark room lined with pillars that pulsed with green glowing energy. Inside the circle of pillars was a wide panel of screens and buttons. "The Nexus." Roark smiled. "All in one concise package. I can practically taste the connection to all those Synthetics." Iskander glared at Roark as he turned to Targ. "Drone, what else needs to be done?"

Targ gulped. He knew his usefulness was coming to an end. "I— uh... have to validate you into the system," he whimpered.

"Make it so," Roark said. Targ slowly walked towards the panel, his knees trembling the closer he got. Roark, Velanna, and Iskander trailed behind him.

"Job's almost done, boss," Velanna said. "You gonna pay up?"

Roark nodded. "You're right. You've done your job well enough." Roark activated a hologram from his palm and accessed a few menus. "The funds should be in your account momentarily."

Velanna looked at the screen on her forearm. Zeros were added to her account in seconds. "Mama likey..." she purred. "Let's finish the job, Papa Hacon."

Targ hesitantly raised his hands to the panel. His eyes darted back and forth, not sure which button was the best one to push first to assist in the genocide of his race.

Suddenly, a metallic ripping sound came from the elevator. Roark slowly turned as Alastor burrowed through the steel floor of the elevator car like a demon climbing out of Hell. He crawled his way up onto his knees before standing up, showing no signs of wear or exhaustion.

"So this is it, son," Roark said. "The moment you've longed for – my death." Alastor unsheathed his sword in silent confirmation.

"Jack, just let it happen," Velanna said. "You're fighting a losing battle." Sparks fell from his armor as Alastor sharpened his sword on the panels of his chest plate.

"Why is it that Ryze, the warlord of these savage machines, is worthy of absolution and mercy, but not your own father?" Roark asked. "After all I've done for you – after all I'm *going* to do for you."

"Ryze didn't kill Melonie," Alastor said with rancor.

Alastor warped straight to his father and swung his sword at him. Roark blocked the attack with the chained blade on his forearm, which was reeled in enough to lock into place. Roark tried to stab Alastor in the side with his blade, but Alastor grabbed his hand and forced it away. He smashed his forehead into Roark's face, breaking his nose, and Roark stumbled backwards as blood leaked from his nostrils. Velanna and Iskander stepped forward to assist, but Roark raised his hand to them. "No. The boy is mine." Roark released the chained blades, each link clinking in quick succession until the steel blade hit the metal ground with a loud clang. "Disciplinary action is far overdue."

"Good," Alastor groaned. "Time for you to finally be a father.

"Are you all alive in there?" Kazt asked over the comms as explosions blasted over the airwaves. Bria, Ryze, and Mason made their way back down the stairs. "Yeah, Alastor's handlin' it. How's the fight?"

"Alastor? Wha–?" Kazt stopped herself. "It's getting rough down here. Taking serious casualties. Not enough supplies to stabilize all of the wounded."

"We will be down shortly," Ryze said. "We have prisoners."

"What's gonna happen to us?" Arashi asked.

"You'll be tried and punished appropriately," Mason said, lugging Malachi's body over his shoulder. "Most likely, you're going to rot in a prison cell for conspiracy to commit a war crime."

The gravity of his consequences began to set in for Arashi. "Does the Council take plea deals?"

Bria's heart twisted. "That's something Melonie would've known." The whole group fell silent.

"Look, if it means anything," Arashi said. "none of us wanted that. That crazy bitch Velanna pulled that shit without Roark's permission."

"Melonie was nice," Sreda muttered. "So sad."

Ryze gasped. "I hate to break up the moment–" He was looking down at the battlefield as Dirt Hounds technicals bounced along the beach, flanking the members of Blur Havok. "Kazt, you have contacts," he told her over the comms.

"They're gonna get chewed up down there," Mason said.

"Take the girl." Ryze dropped Sreda on the stairs and leapt from the stairway into the open beach air. His wings lit up and he threw himself forward with a loud crack as he broke the sound barrier.

"Nothing ever goes accordin' to plan around here..." Bria muttered.

"You've ran from me your whole life!" Alastor's sword clashed with Roark's wrist blade. "And 20 years later, you're still running!"

"I run from no one." Roark punched Alastor in the face and swept his leg with the chain of his blade, tripping Alastor onto his back. Alastor rolled away as Roark pounded his fist into the ground, barely missing his face. He warped to his father and kneed him in the jaw, before upper-cutting him with the armor plating of his knuckles. Roark yelped as he was knocked onto his back, but he recovered quickly and threw out one of his blades. It flew through the air and lodged itself into Alastor's armored chest. Roark pulled his son close and grabbed him by the throat. Alastor drew his 1911 and fired it into Roark's armpit, but only a small amount of blood shot out as he released Alastor. Alastor ripped the blade out of his chest and tossed it away as he fired a bullet into Roark's opposite shoulder. He stumbled back and flung his second blade into Alastor's chest before hauling it over his head, launching Alastor into the air. Roark pulled on the chain, jerking him out of the air and slamming him into the floor. Alastor's sword bounced on the floor next to him, clanging loudly.

"Son," Roark jammed his wrist blade into Alastor's chest as he hoisted him up. "I love you, surely you know this." He raised Alastor up so they were at eye level. "But I will beat you into an unidentifiable pulp before I allow you to smother my lifelong campaign."

Alastor swiped at his father with his metal claws, but Roark blocked them and twisted his arm behind his back. Alastor grunted in pain as he fought against his father. He jabbed Roark in the throat, forcing him to release his hold on him, but his blade stayed planted in his chest. Alastor dove for his sword, the bladed chain whipping and wobbling through the air. Just as he grabbed his sword, Roark yanked Alastor back towards him. He coasted through the air and swung his sword at Roark, only for it to get tangled in his chains. Roark continued to wrap his chains around Alastor's hands, binding him to his sword. He threw his chain around Alastor's shoulders, legs, and waist until he had him constrained in a tightly woven cocoon and, with one swift yank, he tripped Alastor onto his back.

"Give up, boy," Roark said coldly, "and you may possibly still have a seat in the coming empire."

Ryze dove harshly towards the ground. He honed in on the technicals approaching the battle and fired two rockets, blowing three of them up in a fiery explosion. He banked right and landed on the battlefield. Bullets whizzed past his face and soldiers yelled over the sounds of death. A colorful assortment of blood coated the sand of Verfallen

Coast. Ryze dashed to Kazt behind the rocks at the head of the beach.

"Are you okay?" Ryze inspected Kazt. She stared wide-eyed at Ryze and several seconds passed without a response. "Are you going to answer me?" He fired at the Hounds with his machine gun, standing in front of Kazt to block the bullets flying her way.

"I..." Kazt seemed to be lost for words. "I'm fine..." She shook her head to bring herself back to reality. "I'm fine. But our troops aren't as fortunate as me." Ryze was hit in the back by a large caliber bullet that knocked him forward. He flung around and fired his machine gun again, splattering the heads of several Dirt Hounds.

"What are the casualties?"

"At least 3,000, last I heard. Echo, Foxtrot, and Lima squads are MIA." Kazt noticed the crack on Ryze's chest. "You need medical attention."

"Not now." One of the Hound technicals drifted onto the scene, mowing down several Blur Havok troops with the manned turret positioned on the flatbed. Ryze blasted the human on the turret with a rocket, blowing him to smithereens. The truck exploded in a fiery heap, searing the sand beneath. "What's hurting us the most?"

"There's just too many of them, Ryze." Kazt panted breathlessly as she returned to cover and reloaded her built-in submachine gun. "It's attrition warfare. No amount of bombing runs are going to end this fight."

"That's what *you* think." Ryze's wings blasted him into the air, sending sand everywhere.

Bria and Mason made their way down the stairs with their captives. "Ryze left us high and dry up here. Literally," Mason said, holding Sreda by her cuffs.

"He's a better help down there," Bria said as she pulled Arashi behind her. "We just need a way to get out of the front door with all those Hounds in the way." Just as Bria finished her sentence, a group of Dirt Hounds ran up the stairs towards them. "You've got to be shitting me." Bria dropped Arashi on the stairs. "Sit your ass here and don't move." Bria armed herself with her M110 and sniped two of the grunts in the head, splitting their skulls open. "Mason, I'mma need you to start blowin' these bastards up!"

Mason let go of Sreda and began firing his assault rifle at the group. "Ma'am, I don't have too many explosives left." Bodies began piling up on the stairs, but the Hounds kept climbing.

"Fine, but on my signal, you tear ass!" she yelled back, continuously firing at the Hounds while trying to dodge bullets and bludgeons. Dirt Hounds with crowbars, clubs, and baseball bats put serious pressure on the duo as they rushed them.

"This is honestly disturbing," Arashi said as he watched droves of Hounds die. It seemed like a never-ending stream of soldiers.

"Shut it!" Bria yelled as the Hounds got closer. She switched to her MP7 and began rapidly firing at her enemies. Bria looked out to the beach where Ryze was carpet bombing the enemy with rockets, killing large groups of Hounds in multiple fireballs. Bria looked farther along the coast and her heart immediately dropped. More Hounds had come to join the fight. A bullet struck her in the knee, popping a hole in her synthetic leg. Bria screamed as she fell to the floor. She quickly reengaged with the mob while down on one knee. The action of her MP7 flew open. "Mason, explosives – now!"

Mason quickly switched to his grenade launcher and fired two grenades at the horde. They all burst open, leaving a red cloud of blood in the air. The horde was gone, for now. "Good job, Mason." Bria exhaled. In the silence, she heard the sound of faint clicking behind her, gradually getting softer. She turned around to see Sreda fleeing up the stairs, still in handcuffs. Arashi screamed in horror. "Sreda! Stop!"

"Son of a *fuckin' bitch!* "Bria screamed. "Watch Arashi, I'm goin' after her!"

Alastor struggled to break free of the chains. He was unable to warp, as the chains were wrapped tightly around too much of his body. Roark stood over him and placed his taloned foot on Alastor's chest as he turned to address Targ. "What's the progress, drone?" he called out.

"Nearly there," Targ said nervously.

"Speed him up, Velanna." Velanna pressed one of her sharp spider legs against the small of Targ's back and he hastened his pace, if only slightly. Roark turned back to his son. "All of this – the hounding, the betrayal, the accusations of moral impurity, against your *father*, no less. All over a *girl*." Alastor stopped struggling and stared intensely at Roark. His dark, unblinking eyes locked onto Roark's face.

"I told him the sex must have been fantastic to go to these lengths," Velanna added from behind Targ. "Looks like even your old man agrees with me, Jack." Iskander remained silent and watched his brother descend further into madness.

Roark stared at Alastor's ruby red eyes and a small smirk grew on his face. "You're in touch with it. The Warrior's Blood," Roark grumbled. "That raw anger – I've only seen that in my own youth..." Roark studied his son. "Impressive. Unrefined, but impressive nonetheless."

Alastor remained silent, swearing at Roark with his eyes.

"Do you have anything to say for yourself, Alastor?" Roark asked. "Or has your lack of honor blinded you of introspection and inquiry?"

"Arashi told me," Alastor said coldly. "You killed his mother."

"A direct consequence of getting in my way," Roark said, matter-of-factly.

"So it's just dumb luck that you didn't kill my mother, you animal? Did you even care about any of the women you created children with?"

Roark stared somberly into Alastor's hateful eyes. "I loved your mother, son," Roark said as he knelt down. "That is honestly the reason why she lives. I loved her too much to take you from her or to hurt her. But the other ones after her had a usefulness. They created my Knights, the heralds of my blood. Nothing more."

Alastor continued to stare at his father. He glanced at a shocked and appalled Iskander before his eyes slowly slid back to Roark's. After several seconds of nothing but the sound of the battle outside and the rumble of thunder, Alastor finally spoke, his voice gravely and broken. "You're not my father." He paused. "You are an absolute pig," Alastor's voice growled with enough venom to kill an elephant. "And I hate you."

Roark scoffed. A defensive, but clearly feigned smile concealed his pain. "I respect your position. As you will respect mine when you are my age."

"It's ready," Targ said quietly.

"You'll see." Roark stood up and walked away. His chain began dragging the tightly bound Alastor behind him.

Alastor rolled onto his stomach and planted his feet on the ground, standing himself up. He dug himself into the floor and pulled on the chain, yanking Roark back. Roark sneered at Alastor and used all of his synthetic muscles to resist the pull. Alastor's feet slid on the metal floor as he tugged on the chain, but he was not pulling as hard as he could – he was waiting.

Roark groaned to himself. "Your resistance is irritating, boy." He straightened his arm, preparing to yank the chain as hard as he could, but he was doing exactly what Alastor wanted.

Alastor dashed towards Roark right as he yanked on the chain, launching himself through the air. He drove his knee into Roark's face but the momentum catapulted him farther into the air. The chain unraveled and spun Alastor wildly, but within moments, he was free, coasting through the air. He drew his 1911 and fired his handgun directly at Velanna, striking her chest and gut.

He landed across the room with a loud thud. Velanna had fallen to the floor and was grabbing her stomach. Her spider legs autonomously carried her away from Targ and closer to Roark. He stood up and rubbed his jaw. "On your feet," he said to Velanna. "Iskandar, Velanna beat the child down."

Ryze flew through the air, continuing to rain death down upon the Hounds. "Kazt, I'm running low. Coming to you shortly," he said over the comms.

"Take out a few on your way here," Kazt said calmly.

Ryze flew over the battlefield. The amount of Hounds remained consistent while Blur Havok's army was beginning to weaken. "Do we have any reinforcements we can call in?"

"Already on their way. ETA is thirty minutes."

Ryze felt a knot in his throat. "Bria, I need a status report," Ryze said. "The Hounds do not seem to be letting up."

"I'm a little busy right now!" Bria said, panting. "The weird one got away!"

Ryze groaned. "How does this organization even function properly?"

Bria bolted up flights of stairs, chasing after Sreda. "Come back here!" Bria yelled. Sreda continued up the stairs, ignoring her. Bria could hear her panicked breath only meters in front of her. "I *will* shoot you!" Bria called out.

"Dad, help!" Sreda said hastily. "Help!"

"Your dad is an evil bag of dicks!" Bria said. "He's not gonna help you!" Bria was growing more concerned the closer they got to the top as Sreda's capture seemed less achievable the longer the pursuit continued.

Alastor grabbed his sword off the floor and rushed Velanna and Roark. He warped while charging them and reappeared, running full force at Velanna before trampling over her. Alastor swung his sword at Roark, but it clashed with his blade. He spun in the opposite direction and swung his sword again at Roark's unguarded side, but he calmly blocked the second swing.

Velanna crawled away and pressed the chest plate of her armor. An LED menu appeared on her chest: a power symbol, a question mark, and an exclamation point. She slapped the exclamation point and a rotating circle appeared on her chest. "Bullet wound located," a male voice said from her armor. "Cauterizing." The blood that leaked from Velanna's abdomen slowly stopped flowing. "Administering recovery medication," the armor said. "Thanks, Ozzi," she said to herself with a sly smile. Velanna triumphantly shot up onto her spider legs and scurried towards Alastor. He blocked a stab from her spider leg with his sword and stomped down on the joint. She dropped down and Alastor punched her in the face. Velanna stumbled backwards and pulled out her shotgun, firing several slugs at Alastor. He warped to dodge the bullets flying towards him, but a slug hit the blade of his sword and sent it flying out of his hand. Alastor warped straight into the air and kicked Velanna in the gut, sending her straight into the ground.

Alastor drew his 1911 and aimed it at Velanna. Her spider legs were constantly swatting at Alastor, trying to throw off his aim. Alastor grabbed one of the legs and stomped on Velanna's chest. He was about to fire, only to look up and see Roark accessing The Nexus.

Chapter 15

Roark stood at the panel and reached his hand out to it. He shivered as he connected to the millions of lives in The Nexus database. "Yes..." he whispered. "Iskander, we have it. Kill the drone."

Iskander looked at Targ and hesitantly drew his ACR rifle. He took aim at Targ, who cowered and covered his face in a feeble attempt to block the impending gunfire. Iskander could understand the fear in his eyes, but he deactivated the safety on his rifle and blasted five rounds into Targ's stomach. Targ fell backwards down the stairs that had brought them to The Nexus, and his body slumped upside down at the bottom of the stairs as purple blood gushed from his abdomen. He gasped for air as he lay in the growing puddle of his own blood.

A shotgun slug pounded Iskander in the chest and sent him over the panel. Alastor stood over Velanna, holding her shotgun. He pumped it, releasing the spent shell, and aimed at Roark, his finger on the trigger. Roark reached out to Alastor with his open palm and Alastor's lungs suddenly felt tight. He couldn't breathe. He dropped the shotgun and gagged as he fought to draw air into his mouth. He clutched at his chest and fell to his knees beside Velanna.

Suddenly, he could breathe again and Alastor inhaled sharply, only for his lungs to squeeze again, cutting off his breath. Alastor fell onto his side.

"You will breathe when I say you can breathe." Roark smirked and turned back to the panel. "Valhalla, your cleansing awaits."

The fight showed no signs of ending as Ryze flew over the warring beach towards Kazt. His heart palpitated and his wings sputtered before completely shutting off. "What—?" he grunted as he fell from the sky. A sharp, wailing sound came from his wings as Ryze spiraled to the ground, his vision blurred as the world around him spun. His body hammered into the sandy beach and he tumbled through the sand in a flailing heap of massive limbs. His crash landing killed several Hounds in his path, splattering them across the sand. Ryze came to a stop on his back, mere feet from Kazt.

"Ryze?" Kazt called out. She ran to her leader, only to feel her heart stutter in her chest. She screamed out and fell to her knees, collapsing over Ryze's chest. "Ryze, what's ha—?" she grunted as she watched Ryze's eyes flicker.

"The Nexus," Ryze muttered. Static was woven into his voice as he spoke. "He's inside..." His heart felt like it was about to physically explode. Ryze turned his head to find droves of Ski'tal beginning to falter, collapsing mid-combat and Blur Havok members running to check on them.

"Bria, we're dying..." Ryze said weakly. "Roark is winning..."

"Ryze! Hang in there!" Bria yelled as she continued to chase after Sreda. The duo reached the platform that led to The Nexus chamber and Bria tackled Sreda in front of the elevator. She squirmed and fought against Bria. "Hold still, you crazy motherfucker!"

"I must help dad!" Sreda said again. "He needs help!"

"That is the last thing he needs!"

"Bria..." Ryze said over the comms.

"I know – dying. Trying to help!" Bria said as she tussled with Sreda.

"No. Help is here."

A man cleared his voice over the comms. "Is this thing on?"

Bria pinned Sreda down by holding her wrists above her head. "Ozzi?" she exhaled.

"Yes! Figured out the frequency faster than I thought."

"Where are you?"

"I'm close enough," Ozzi replied. "And I brought toys. Well, one toy, actually. It's quite big."

On the beach, a towering, tracked vehicle bounced across the sand. It was a fourth the height of The Nexus and several cannons protruded from the top of the looming machine, telescoping and pointing to the sky. Its metal-plated hull adjusted and shifted to protect its inner components as it slowed to a halt at the head of the beach.

"Is that..." Ryze struggled to speak. "...the superweapon..." he groaned, wincing as he spoke. "...from The Vault?"

"In the steel-armored flesh," Ozzi said from the cockpit of the vehicle. "Now, if I recall correctly, this thing is quite the picky eater." Ozzi played with the switches and dials in the cockpit. "Bypassing all Ski'tal and remaining Blur Havok members via frequencies. Designating traitors and Dirt Hounds." The Dirt Hounds disengaged from battle and stared at the enormous machination in awe. Some fired upon the metal beast, but their attacks were futile.

Ozzi stopped pecking at the keys and buttons. He inhaled and slowly exhaled, as a vengeful smile grew on his lips. "Eat shit." Ozzi pressed a large green button. The monstrous vehicle groaned, bellowing deeply and shaking the ground. Half of the barrels on the vehicle pointed to the sky, the other half pointed at the Dirt Hounds on the ground. A loud clunk came from within the apparatus and all hell broke loose.

Bullets fired down at the Dirt Hounds, flattening their soft bodies as fire shot from the barrels, catapulting into the sky before falling to the Earth. The meteors screamed as they fell from the sky and crashed into the beach. Hounds that weren't penetrated by bullets were obliterated, bludgeoned, and incinerated by searing fires from the explosives. They looked like ants scattering desperately across the beach.

"I christen thee, Azrael," Ozzi said darkly. He watched as the enemy was eviscerated by the unconquerable force of the superweapon. He looked at his right arm, which had been replaced with a fully synthetic and unskinned arm. "For Melonie," he said softly to himself, sorrow filling his voice.

Blood dripped from Roark's nose as he stood at The Nexus. The connection to millions of lives was taxing him far greater than his body could take. Alastor was on his back, yards away, struggling to breathe as Roark continued to disable his synthetic lungs. Tears leaked from Alastor's eyes as he fought to stay alive. Velanna rolled onto her stomach, panting as she collected herself. "You're a good fight, Jack," Velanna said, breathing heavily. "We could be absolutely unstoppable, babe..."

Iskander stumbled to his feet. The sight of Roark torturing Alastor appalled him. "Enough," he said.

Roark coughed and blood shot from his mouth. "Goodbye, my sons," he grunted. "I leave you the riches of Valhalla."

Three loud steps approached Roark and Iskander suddenly rammed him, sending him flying away from The Nexus panel. Alastor gasped and greedily heaved in air.

Ryze jerked, barely alive. The black clouds above him glowed orange as fire dove from the sky. It looked as though God had unleashed his wrath upon Verfallen Coast. Ryze looked at his chest where Kazt lay across his breast. She coughed back to life and her blue eyes stared up at Ryze. Her diamond-shaped face was youthful and vibrant, and her vivid yellow cloud of hair ran down the back of her head, behind the crescent headpiece that adorned her forehead.

"Are you okay?" Ryze asked. He stared at her, wide-eyed with a dazzled expression on his face. It was the first time he had truly paid attention to Kazt's face.

Kazt smiled slightly. "Never better."

Bria hauled Sreda to her feet and looked outside of The Nexus. The flaming breaths falling from the heavens fell parallel to The Nexus walls. "Holy shit, Ozzi!" Bria laughed. "Way to go!"

"Bria, I'm on my way!" Ryze said over the comms, his voice vibrant.

"Roark must be out of The Nexus!" Bria gasped. "We're winning!"

Sreda gawked at the hellscape around her. Bria's words and the sight of her father's plans *literally* burning before her eyes made Sreda panic. She glanced down at Bria's leg and sharply jabbed her bladed limb into her shin, tearing into the synthetic skin on her leg.

"Son of a bitch!" Bria yelled as she stumbled away. Sreda ran towards the elevator and jumped into the shaft. She used her cuffed hands and the pointed tips of her legs to climb the walls. Bria stood up and tried to run after her, but she stumbled forward, limping. She grabbed her damaged leg and groaned. "That is one weird, slippery little girl."

"This ends now, dad!" Iskander called out boldly.

Roark was weakened by The Nexus' toll on his body and blood leaked from the side of his mouth. "Now *you* have betrayed me? My most trusted son?"

"I've stood by long enough, letting your evil reign!" Iskander rushed at his father but Roark simply raised his hand to him. Iskander fell to the floor and tumbled towards Roark, but he managed to grab his father and tackle him in the momentum, sending the two rolling across the floor in a large mess.

Alastor used his sword to stand back up but Velanna immediately swiped it away from him and he fell to the floor, his battle-masked face smacking against the metal surface. "None of this matters, Jack." Velanna stood over him. "This is just the first step." Alastor swiped at Velanna's leg and tripped her up. She slammed onto her back and Alastor quickly scrambled on top of her, savagely clawing at her armor and ripping it apart as she covered her face. Velanna batted Alastor off of her with one of her spider legs. Her mechanical appendages helped her up as plates and pieces of armor were shed off of her. "My Prince Charming..." Velanna said sarcastically.

Iskander threw Roark across the room. He grabbed his claymore and it unfolded as he strode towards his father. "You watched Malachi die and did *nothing*!" Iskander thrust his massive sword at Roark, but he deflected it.

"He paid the price. He failed me." Roark stabbed Iskander in the leg with his chained blade and Iskander fell onto his injured knee. "As have you," Roark said as he backhanded Iskander.

"I don't care!" Iskander grabbed Roark by the throat and raised him off of his feet. "I am done fighting your battles for you," Iskander said. "I am done with you and this war!" Iskander smashed his father into the floor, denting it. Roark yanked the chain attached to Iskander's leg and flipped him backwards. Iskander landed on his back with a large boom.

"This is the hard part, Jack." Velanna used her legs to block Alastor's sword as he swiped at her furiously. "It only gets easier from here if you just *cooperate* "

Alastor warped behind Velanna and bashed his heel into the small of her knee. She buckled to the floor and he rushed at her, holding his sword to her neck. Velanna's spider legs burst from her back, pushing Alastor across the room. She quickly turned to Alastor and dashed at him, pulling out her shotgun. She blasted several slugs at him, pumping the gun after each round, but Alastor dodged them all. Velanna blasted one last shell at Alastor and he dodged the slug with a warp. He reappeared directly in front of her and, with the righteous efficiency of a samurai, Alastor twirled his sword and sliced Velanna's right hand off. She screamed as her armored hand and shotgun plopped onto the floor, dark red blood squirting from the wound. Her insect legs scurried her into the dark corners of the shadows, disappearing into the blackness.

Alastor slowly turned to watch as Iskander and Roark continued their struggle. Alastor began to run at his father, and each step was like the deep, ominous pounding of his internal war drum.

Velanna crept out of the darkness, losing a large amount of blood. The armor could not heal a wound of this size. She spotted her shotgun and grabbed it with her remaining hand. Her weapon was still piping hot and she pressed the barrel against her bleeding stump. She screeched as the searing metal crudely cauterized the wound. Velanna dropped the empty shotgun. She heard the scraping of metal coming from the elevator as Sreda climbed through the hole Alastor had burrowed. She frantically breached the opening and rolled onto her back. "Sreda," Velanna said. "It's good to see you, friend."

Alastor ran at Roark and warped into the air as Iskander pushed away from him. Roark looked up and saw Alastor gliding through the air with his sword cocked back, ready to pierce Roark's chest with his blade. He quickly reeled his own blade back and, in one swift and fluid motion, Roark bashed the broad side of his blade against Alastor's sword and caught him by the throat. Alastor's blade shattered into pieces, leaving only a few jagged teeth on the hilt. "I am no dreg, boy," Roark said. "Your simple techniques are farcical.

Ryze flew up the stairs towards Bria, who sat on the ground clutching her shin. He quickly landed on the platform before the main Nexus chamber and approached her. "What happened? Where is the girl?" he asked.

"Oh no, don't worry about *me*. I'm fine," Bria said with scathing sarcasm. Ryze's lips shifted, realizing that he sounded rather callous.

"She climbed up the elevator shaft," Bria continued. "Where's Mason?"

"He and Arashi made it off of Verfallen Coast. They're with Kazt now."

"Good," Bria sighed. "That's my nigga."

"Ozzi is forcing the Dirt Hounds to flee and we've got reinforcements inbound. The fight is almost over."

Bria narrowed her eyes. "Fight's not over till I know my bro's safe."

Ryze wanted to object but, truthfully, he found Bria to be a worthy ally in this moment. "I respect that." Ryze nodded, accepting Bria's camaraderie. "Come. I'll help you up." Ryze offered his hand and Bria smiled as she placed her hand in his.

"Uh, guys?" Ozzi said over the comms.

"Yeah?" Bria said, her voice strained.

"A miscalculation just occurred," Ozzi said with trepidation.

"What exactly do you mean?" Ryze said, trying to stay calm.

"There's some red hot bad news falling from the sky." Ozzi paused. "Take cover."

"Oh crap," Bria muttered.

Alastor dropped his broken sword, letting it clang loudly against the metal floor as he hung from his father's trembling grasp. Roark threw Alastor into the ground, leaving a small crater in the steel. "I no longer have the energy to toy with you children," Roark croaked.

Iskander slammed the butt of his rifle into Roark's head, sending him lurching forward and releasing Alastor from his grip. Alastor looked up at Iskander as he held his hand out to help him up. His crimson eyes stared at Iskander's open hand. He looked back up at him and slapped his hand into Iskander's. "Let's finish this," Iskander said.

Roark fell to the floor weakly, stumbling as he tried to stand up. His armor was damaged and broken. "Velanna!" he called out, blood leaking from every hole on his face. "Come to me!" he said as he reached his hand out. Suddenly, a resounding eruption came from above and the ceiling ripped open in a flaming blossom. The stormy night sky appeared past the rift and the crisp ocean wind blew through The Nexus' chamber. The green energized rods shot emerald bolts of energy into the sky, arcing wildly in the stormy air.

Velanna stood by Sreda. "We need to retreat," Velanna said.

Sreda gasped softly. "But my father—!"

"Call it," Velanna interrupted her. "It's all on you now. I've got contacts that will help us get out of here."

Sreda watched her father crawl weakly across the floor as Alastor and Iskander approached him.

"You'll pay for what you've done, father," Iskander said. He grabbed Roark's hair and pulled him to his feet. Roark swatted Iskander's hand away and threw one of his blades towards Alastor, the chains rattling as they flew through the air.

Alastor warped to Roark and punched him in the gut. Roark fell to his knees, only for Alastor to knee him in the face, sending him reeling backwards. Blood flew out of

Roark's mouth and arced through the air as he fell onto his back with a brutal thud, his crimson headpiece clanging on the ground next to him. Iskander swung his claymore down on his father's legs, slicing the synthetic limbs at the knee. Roark threw his head back and screamed out in pain.

Sreda watched in horror as her father was ripped apart piece by piece in front of her very eyes.

Bria and Ryze tumbled around as The Nexus was bombarded with artillery fire. “Ozzi, stop this shit!” Bria called out.

“I'm trying, but the system is hard locked!” Ozzi replied over the comms. “This experimental tech hasn't even been beta tested!”

“Oh, no.” Bria rolled towards the edge of the platform, sliding uncontrollably towards a huge drop. Ryze leapt to Bria, but she rolled off of the edge. He jumped off the platform and flew straight down, catching her in his arms. He swiftly curved back up and flew parallel to The Nexus.

“Holy shit, that was wild,” Bria said. She shakily climbed onto Ryze's back and held on tight. “Good lookin' out, Ryze.”

“Don't mention it,” Ryze said assuredly. “We're going after Alastor.”

“Hell yeah!” Bria yelled jubilantly.

Fire continued to rain from above as The Nexus pulsed viridescent electricity into the blackened heavens, coating the clouds in an unholy green and orange glow.

"I need a lift," Velanna said to someone over the comms. "Yeah, you already know where I am. Sending exact coordinates." Velanna glared at Sreda. "Call the retreat!" she yelled. The Nexus continued to shake and rumble. As Sreda continued to watch, she began her compulsive rhythm.

Click. Tick, tick, tock.

Click. Tick, tick, tock.

Click. Tick, tick —

Velanna slapped Sreda's hands. "Snap out of it! Now is not the time!" Sreda curled into a ball, tears welling up in her eyes.

Roark rolled over onto his side, coughing up copious amounts of blood. Alastor slowly walked over to him. Only his demonic red eyes were visible behind his battle mask. He stared at his dying father, wallowing in his own blood. Alastor slowly pressed the heel of his steel foot onto Roark's throat and drew his 1911. He cocked the hammer and slowly aligned the barrel of his pistol with Roark's head. "Goodbye, Roark," Alastor said softly.

Suddenly, Roark threw his left arm forward, sending his chained blade towards Alastor. In mere nanoseconds, Alastor dodged the blade and grabbed the chain before it had even passed his head. He twisted around and plunged the chained blade deep into Roark's chest. Blood burst from the wound and Roark gurgled loudly on his own blood.

"Dad!" Sreda screamed out. She ran to her father, but Velanna tackled her. Sreda clawed the hard floor, scraping her synthetic claws against the metal. "No! No! No!" she pleaded.

Velanna struggled to hold Sreda back with her one hand. Her spider limbs shot out and grabbed the torn ledge of the flaming hole and pulled the pair away from the dying Roark. A black VTOL swiftly and quietly swooped to the top of the tower and lowered its ramp. "Fine, I'll do it myself." Velanna tossed Sreda into the VTOL. "This is Velanna speaking," she said over the comms. "I'm issuing a full retreat! Roark is down!" Velanna jumped onto the VTOL. "The mission is a failure. Rendezvous at broadcasted coordinates. Anyone left is a dead man."

Alastor looked up from his bleeding father and his eyes met Velanna's. She had her back half turned, ready to leave, but she had waited. A knowing, nefarious smirk spread across her face. Velanna looked to her right as Bria and Ryze appeared from the elevator shaft. Without saying a word, she turned away and the VTOL ramp closed.

"There she is!" Bria hopped off of Ryze's back and aimed her M110 at Velanna, only for Ryze to place his hand on the barrel of her sniper rifle and slowly lower it as

Velanna's scout vehicle flew off into the midst of raining fire. Bria looked at Ryze, confused, only to see him solemnly pointing at the slain Roark in Alastor's hands.

Alastor slowly looked back at his father on his deathbed. Blood bubbled in his mouth as he tried to speak. "Alastor..." Roark said. He weakly slapped his hand against Alastor's chest, leaving a streak of blood. "Why did *you* —?"

Alastor felt as though his heart was ripping in half. He yanked the blade from Roark's chest and blood spurted from the wound. Alastor's fingers rolled off of Roark's body, letting him drop to the floor. Roark let out one last death rattle before his head lulled to the side. He held Roark's blade in his hand, panting from holding his breath the entire time. Iskander placed a hand on his armored shoulder. Alastor stared off into the stormy horizon, and the sound of thunder grumbled in the distance as artillery fire continued to fall from the sky.

But no tears fell from Alastor's eyes.

You are not alone.

If you or someone you know is experiencing depression or thoughts of suicide, call the National Suicide Prevention Lifeline at 1-800-273-8255 (US) or 116 123 (UK) at any time.